Death
in the
Old Country

Also available in Large Print
by Eric Wright:

Smoke Detector

Death in the Old Country

An Inspector Charlie Salter Mystery

Eric Wright

G.K.HALL&CO.
Boston, Massachusetts
1986

Published in Large Print by arrangement with
New American Library

G.K. Hall Large Print Book Series

Set in 16 pt Plantin

Library of Congress Cataloging in Publication Data

Wright, Eric.
  Death in the old country.

  (G.K. Hall large print book series)
  1. Large type books. I. Title.
[PR9199.3.W66D4 1986]   813'.54   85-27191
ISBN 0-8161-3966-0 (lg. print)

For Maurice Elliott

One

Life in the Old Country

At three o'clock on a rainy afternoon in early May, Charlie Salter was driving in heavy two-way traffic on a narrow country road, keeping plenty of space between him and the car in front, happy that for once the conditions were so bad that no one was trying to overtake him as he led a procession of cars at a safe speed across the middle of England. He was enjoying himself, pleased with his miniature rented car, and very nearly comfortable with being on the wrong side of the road. Beside him, his wife, Annie, was reading a guide-book.

Before long they would have to choose where they were going to stay the night, a problem that could generate enough tension between them to last well into the evening, especially if the dinner was bad. The Salters were Canadian, used to travelling on a con-

1

tinent of standardized motels with restaurants attached which provided standardized meals from dawn to midnight. In England, they had discovered, you could find yourself at five o'clock in the afternoon in a village where the teashop was closed and there was no room at the inn; this was a land where the natives did not set foot out of doors without an exchange of stamped, addressed envelopes reserving their accommodation months in advance. On several afternoons already they had agonized as they tried to guess whether there might not be somewhere more inviting 'just round the next bend', passing up the 'Bed and Breakfast' sign outside the local Wuthering Heights as they searched for an inn with mullioned windows, a fire roaring in the hearth, and a jolly host waiting with a steaming bowl of bishop for his damp and weary guests.

Annie's instinct was always to stop, unless they had had a bad experience the night before, when she became single-minded in the pursuit of comfort, determined on a five-star hotel at a hundred guineas a night, if necessary. Salter tended to drive on, 'just to the next town', not even checking anything that looked less than perfect. And so they beat on (since he was usually driving), getting more irritated as they became more worried. If, after an hour of this, they did stumble on somewhere good, the relief was so enormous that they heaped credit on each other for finding the place; if they settled in despair on somewhere bad, the best they could manage was an elaborate politeness as each rose selflessly above the desire to blame the other.

All this was an hour away, however, and Salter gave himself up to meditating contentedly about the rain. How many words did the English have for it? 'Spitting', 'drizzling', 'a few drops', 'damp out' – these were a few of them. And it *was* different. Salter was used to rain, real rain, that had been forecast, that had a beginning and an ending and then left you alone for a few weeks. This rain, though, did not so much fall as hang in the air, silently enveloping the world and soaking it to the skin.

The road curved to the left following a high stone wall which protected the local stately home from being looked at by tourists in rented cars. As they chugged along in their little sealed chamber, daydreaming in the quiet time when the stationary world is having a nice nap, the road straightened, and Salter heard, first, the sound of a woman screaming, then saw, through the mist, a motorcycle and sidecar combination coming at him out of control on his side of the road. The woman was riding on the pillion, and the driver, a small hunched figure in a black overcoat and a green helmet, was trying to point his wheel out of the skid. Salter had all the time in the world to pull in as close to the wall as he could and come to a dead stop before the sidecar smashed into him with a noise of splintering wood.

Salter unbuckled and stepped out into the rain as the motorcyclist disentangled himself. Gradually the woman's screams wound down as she realized she was alive, and she fell silent. Three small boys clambered from the wreckage of the sidecar, a do-it-yourself contraption of plywood and two-by-fours, and all parties tested themselves for injuries. No one seemed to be hurt, so Salter and the motorcyclist began to square off.

A woman with a coat over her head ran towards them across the fields on the right. 'Oi seed it all,' she cried as she ran. 'Oi seed it all. Oi've already notified the police and the ambularances.' She arrived at the car breathless, and repeated her message. Salter broke off his conversation with the motor-cyclist, who was shaking his head and saying, 'Coming at a fair lick, wasn't you? A fair lick?' as he established his opening defence.

The traffic was stopped for some distance in both directions and Salter approached the driver of the car behind him.

'Did you see what happened?' he asked the man. His car had been glued in Salter's rear-view mirror for the last five miles.

'No, not properly,' the man said. 'Like, not to be sure, I mean.'

'Oh, you did see it, Les, didn't you,' his wife said. 'I mean, you can't deny it. You did see it all. It wasn't this gentleman's fault. I mean, you did see it, didn't you.'

'Oh, bloody hell,' the man said. 'All right. Here's my name and address. I can't give evidence, though, not in person. I'm on me 'olidays.'

'Still,' his wife said, 'you did see it.'

Salter looked around for more witnesses, but the other drivers were back in their cars, avoiding his eye.

Two police constables appeared: one, dark-haired and dapper with a moustache, the other fair and clean-shaven. They quickly began the process of sorting out the scene. The accident was so clear-cut — the motorcycle had been trying to overtake a stream of traffic on a blind curve — that Salter could see the concern of the police shift quickly from establishing responsibility to deciding whether to lay a charge against the motorcyclist. It was time to pull rank. He approached the dark-haired constable and showed him a second piece of identification and suggested that while the motorcyclist was obviously at fault, it really was an accident. 'Besides,' he added, 'I'm on my holidays.'

The constable called to his colleague and showed him Salter's identification. 'Ah well, then,' the colleague said. 'We'll have this sorted out in no time then, won't we, Inspector?'

The motorcyclist turned to his wife. 'He's a bleedin' copper,' he said. 'Just our luck.'

Annie, who had been standing by the car under an umbrella, appeared beside them. 'What's happening, Charlie?' she asked. 'Those poor people are getting soaked.' She motioned to the motorcyclist's family who were huddled together by the wreck of their vehicle. 'Get into our car while they sort this out,' she said to the woman. 'At least you and the children.'

'Oh no! We'll make your car all wet!' the woman cried.

'It's wet now. Please get in,' Annie insisted.

'Yes, well, all right, then. If you are sure your husband won't mind,' the woman said, and squeezed herself and the three boys into the back of the car. Two breakdown trucks arrived, and the whole group was transported to a garage in the local town, where hot tea was provided while they assessed the damage. For such a slight collision, the damage turned out to be considerable. 'I think you've bent the frame,' the garage proprietor said. 'Take us two weeks. Easy.'

Salter arranged for a fresh car to be delivered from the rental agency the next day, feeling fat with the knowledge that he had paid an extra two pounds a day to insure himself to the hilt. 'Now,' he said to the two policemen. 'We need a place to stay. Any suggestions?'

'P'raps we might go down to the station,' the dark-haired constable suggested. 'My inspector would like to meet you, I'm sure, and he'll know the best places.'

'Right,' Salter said. 'What about them?' He indicated the motorcyclist and his family, now sitting in a row on a bench against the wall, each with a bag of potato crisps.

'We'll look after them,' the constable replied. 'They're Londoners. They'll have to go on by rail, and there's no train until seven. Got no money, of course, but we'll take care of them one way or another.'

'Where are we, by the way?' Salter asked. 'What town, I mean?'

'This is Tokesbury Mallett, sir,' the constable said, surprised. 'Now, if you and your wife will come with me – oh yes, luggage – right you are, then. We'll be off. See you later, Robbo,' he called to the fair constable who was filling in forms with the proprietor.

Tokesbury Mallett was made entirely of the local yellow stone, and the buildings in the high street might have existed for five hundred years. The entrance to the police station was at the end of a row of shops, through an arch over the cobbled driveway of a large inn. Apart from the discreet blue lamp over the door, the station was indistinguishable from its olde worlde neighbours. The constable led them inside and introduced them to a sergeant sitting behind a counter, who shook hands with Salter and nodded to the constable to take them through to an inner office which overlooked the high street. Here, a thin, flat-haired man in a tweed suit with a handkerchief in his breast pocket sat writing at a desk.

The room smelled strongly of furniture polish. On one wall, an ordnance survey map of the area was decorated in military fashion with little flags and coloured pins. Beside it was a chart on graph paper on which a line ended in mid-air. It was too far away for Salter to read what was being charted. Rainfall? Behind the desk another large board displayed some kind of duty roster carefully picked out in three colours of ink. The highly polished desk sported a silver inkstand with two small crystal bottles of ink, one red, one green, an IN-tray and an OUT-tray, and a blotting-pad with edges of gold-embossed leather.

'This is Inspector Churcher, sir,' the constable said, 'and *this* is Inspector Salter, sir, from the Toronto police. In Canada, sir. He was in a head-on collision on the Oxford road, nobody hurt, other party liable.'

'And his wife, I assume,' Churcher said,

9

rising to shake hands with Salter and smile at Annie. 'Please sit down.' He waited until Annie was in contact with her chair and sat down himself. 'A bit grubby, I'm afraid—a working office. Nasty thing to happen on holiday, Inspector, but I am very glad to have the opportunity to meet a colonial colleague. What can we do to make up for your trouble? Cup of tea?'

'No, thanks. Tell us where to find a bed,' Salter said. 'And where to get something to eat, later.'

Churcher ran a smoothing hand over his neat haircut, and sat at attention. His hands moved to settle his tie in the centre of his shirt-front and to equalize the exposed portion of his shirt-cuffs. He screwed his fountain-pen together and laid it in the tray of the inkstand.

'Now, I'm a bit new here,' he said. 'But, we do boast a two-star establishment, the Swan. Then there's the Jolly Alderman. And there are any number of smaller places. Hang on a second. Sergeant!' he called, through the open door. 'Come and join us for a moment. Sergeant Robey is a local man,' he explained to Salter. 'Ah, Sergeant. This is Inspector Salter, a colleague from the

Dominions, and his wife. They need lodgings for the night. What do you suggest?' He looked keenly, first at the sergeant, then at Salter, then back at the sergeant.

'I want somewhere dry and warm with a decent bed and lots of hot water,' Salter said.

'And no restrictions on the use of the bathroom,' said Annie, whose teeth were starting to chatter. 'We don't care if there's no television, and we've got our own whisky so it doesn't have to be licensed, but it would be nice if they would give us something to eat so that we don't have to go out again in this weather.'

'You want Boomewood, ma'am,' the sergeant said.

'Oh, surely not, Sergeant,' Churcher protested. 'I don't think it's even rated, is it? Hardly appropriate.' He smiled at Salter and Annie.

'Binks, who runs the Swan, is on the fiddle, especially with foreigners,' the sergeant replied. 'And I wouldn't serve the food at the Jolly Alderman to my dog.' He turned to Salter. 'Frozen faggotts and peas,' he said. 'And tinned rice pudd'n for afters.'

Salter, not sure he had heard right, nevertheless felt himself in good hands. 'Boomewood it is, then,' he said. 'Anything wrong with it that you know of, Inspector?' he asked politely.

Churcher, irritated at the immediate understanding that had sprung up between Salter and his sergeant, shrugged. 'Don't let me put you off,' he said. 'But I think we'd better give him fair warning, Sergeant, don't you?'

'I was going to, sir.' The sergeant turned again to the Salters. 'There's been a report there's been a prowler there, sir. An Indian lady staying there a few days ago complained that someone woke her up in the night. This prowler was tickling her foot, saying "wakey-wakey". She sat up and he did a bunk, sir. She never screamed or nothing, very collected she was. She was sharing the room with her daughter, you see. They were on a motoring holiday before the daughter went to college, and the Indian lady didn't want to alarm her daughter, but she went to the landlord and told him. The next day she came to us because she thought the landlord wasn't taking it serious enough. We investigated, of course, but it was a waste of time. In my opinion a couple of the other guests had arranged a bit of slap and tickle — excuse me, ma'am – and he'd got the room number wrong. You know what I mean? But it's a nice place, and the locals say they've got good grub, if you like Italian. I do,' he added.

'Oh God, Charlie,' Annie exclaimed. 'Let's go.'

'Right you are, then,' Churcher said, attempting to take over. 'And if anyone grabs you by the ankle in the night, apart from your wife, I mean, hang on to him until we get there, will you?' He laughed to show he was joking. 'I'll get Potter to drive you.'

'I'll take them, sir,' Sergeant Robey offered. 'I'm just going off duty.'

'Right you are, then,' Churcher said again. He shook hands with Salter. 'Do come in tomorrow morning before you leave. I'd enjoy a little chat with a colleague from the New World. Now take this poor lady off and find her a nice hot bath, Sergeant. I'll telephone Boomewood to expect you.'

Salter said, 'Would you mind not mentioning that I'm a colleague of yours? From the New World. It makes people nervous. I'm calling myself a maintenance supervisor from the Toronto Transit Commission.'

'Ha, ha, ha. Your cover, eh?' Churcher

13

said. 'Right you are, then. Mum's the word.'

And bob's your uncle, thought Salter. And keep your pecker up. And cheery-bye, then. 'Thanks,' he said.

In the car, the sergeant said, 'I spoke up because the inspector's a bit new to the district, sir. He doesn't know what a rotten hole the Swan is. Now.' He turned a corner and stopped the car with the engine running. 'If it ever stops raining and you feel like a walk, there's the best pub in the town.' He pointed across the street to a sign, the Eagle and Child, above the door. A single lighted window, as from a cottage, was the only other evidence of life. 'It's warm, cosy, *and* the beer's good.'

'Sergeant,' Annie called from the back seat. 'How far is Boomewood?'

'Half a mile, ma'am.' He looked round and registered a white, pinched face. 'Sorry, ma'am,' he said. 'You're cold. I'll have you there in a jiffy.'

He turned right, down a street lined with shops, past an intersection, and pulled up by a row of large attached houses with square windows and doors that opened directly on to the pavement. At one time, Salter guessed, these were residences for fops in wigs. Now,

14

most of them had been taken over by auctioneers and chartered surveyors, but outside one a discreet plate announced that it was 'Boomewood – Private Hotel'.

'What does "Private" mean?' Salter asked.

'It means they don't have a public bar,' the sergeant said. 'They do have drinks, though, for the guests, and wine in the dining-room.'

He helped them carry their luggage into the narrow hallway where they were met by a slightly plump woman who was evidently not English, though Salter was not sure why he thought so. She was in her late thirties: dark, creamy complexion; brown hair pulled back and held behind her head; dark woollen dress with a cardigan round her shoulders; and elegant, nearly non-existent shoes that made her feet look nice and were the opposite of sensible. It was the shoes, Salter decided, that gave her away.

'Hello, Sergeant,' she said, touching him on the arm. 'No problems for you today.' She laughed as if she had made a good joke. Her accent was Italian.

Robey looked pleased with himself. 'This is Mr and Mrs Salter,' he said. 'The inspector called, did he, Mrs Dillon?'

She nodded and smiled. 'We are waiting

for you,' she said. 'A double with a bath-room.' She moved forward to bring her arm around Annie and make her the centre of the group. 'If you would sign the register, Mr Salter, I will show your wife the room,' she said, leading Annie away and up the stairs.

'I'll be off, then, sir,' the sergeant said. 'You'll call in tomorrow, will you? The inspector would like it if you would. He's very keen on exchanging ideas.' The sergeant's face was bland.

'I'm just a layman,' Salter reminded him clearly. 'But I'll be happy to let him know that I think his policemen are wonderful.'

'That's it, sir. That's the sort of thing he likes to hear.'

Thus, with no more than a couple of in-flections, did the sergeant confirm Salter's impression that Inspector Churcher was not only new, but zealous, uncertain of himself, and perhaps a trifle silly. Poor bugger, thought Salter.

'This way, please,' Mrs Dillon called.

Salter's hopes rose as they climbed the stairs which were lined with ancient pho-tographs of sunny foreign landscapes. They rose further when he saw the room: a huge, solid-looking bed, two armchairs, a view of

16

the rain-soaked hills from the window, and heat coming from the radiators. The bathroom, also, was heated, and it contained a giant's bath, a shower, a shaving light, and at least six— count 'em, he thought, six— thick-looking towels. One more test. Salter switched on one of the bedside lamps and a light bright enough to read by came on. They wouldn't need the hundred-watt bulb they carried around with them on the advice of a friend experienced in English hotels.

'This'll do,' he said to the waiting woman.

'Our best *camera matrimoniale*,' she said.

'What?'

'Double room.' She smiled, and left.

Salter took off his shoes and sat on the bed to test it. 'You think we've been asking for the right thing?' he called out to Annie, who was already running the bath. *'Camera matrimoniale* is what we wanted. You think they are all like this in Italy?'

'Don't be silly, Charlie.' Annie stepped into the tub and slid under the surface, whimpering with pleasure. After a few seconds she adjusted herself so that the water came to her chin. 'We just got lucky, that's all. Pour me a drink.'

17

Salter, now half-undressed himself, dug out the bottle of Scotch that their experienced friend had advised them to carry with them at all times in England, found two tooth-glasses, and measured out the drinks. He took off the rest of his clothes and sat on a towel on the edge of the bathtub with his feet in the water.

'I wish I smoked,' Annie said. 'Then I could have it all.'

'There's room for me in there,' Salter said, pointing to the nearly half of the tub which lay beyond Annie's feet.

'No, there isn't. Wait your turn.' She sipped her drink. 'Can we have dinner here? Should we?'

'The sergeant said they cook. All the evidence says we should try it.' He reached into the water, pulled out one of her feet, and began using the toes for counter. 'One, it's warm. Two, there's hot water—lots of it. Three, the bed has a proper mattress. Four, you can read in bed. Five, the owner, Mrs Whatever, looks well-fed, and has an Italian accent.'

She pulled her foot away as he tickled first her ankle, then behind her knee. 'Six,' she said, 'it's pouring with rain. Seven, I can

18

smell garlic.' She stood up. 'Your turn,' she said.

Salter topped the bath with more hot water and lowered himself in. 'Ah-ah-ah-ah-' he said.

When he had soaked enough, he dried himself slowly and moved into the bedroom, where he found Annie with a towel wrapped around her head, fast asleep under the eiderdown. He poured himself another drink, draped himself in one of the enormous bath-towels (don't bother with dressing-gowns, their experienced friend had said, use your raincoats; so far he was batting about five hundred) and sat in an armchair, gazing out across the roofs to the fields and hills of the home of his fathers.

They had been travelling for a week, the first of a planned four-week holiday touring England and Scotland. After a long, cold, Toronto winter, and a bad patch in their marriage, the Salters had decided on a major change of scene and rhythm. They had both been working hard, Annie especially, absorbed in her new career in an advertising agency. Salter had been slow to adjust to the new pattern demanded by her job, a life of more restaurant meals than usual, occasional

19

dinners assembled at a delicatessen by Annie on her way home, and even more occasionally, Salter, alone, cooking grilled cheese sandwiches for himself and the two boys. Several times on a Saturday Annie had been involved in setting up a 'shoot', and Salter had been left to mooch about by himself. The intervals between their love-making lengthened because of tiredness and because an irritation between them had turned into a wall when they retired. Then, in February, Annie had decided to finish with child-bearing. She was approaching forty, the boys were ten and fourteen, and they agreed it was now too late for another child. All this made sense to Salter, but he nevertheless endured a small sadness because of it. He loved his sons, but he got on with them less well than Annie did. Father and sons were wary of each other. When he looked at colleagues with daughters, he envied slightly what looked like a much simpler relationship, and he thought he would have liked a little girl around. But he did not crave another son, and besides, the timing had never been right. When Annie came back from hospital after the operation, he imagined a new fragility about her that created another barrier. Salter, typically, tried to ignore the problem that seemed to be developing but when Annie's job was secure, she carved a gap in her schedule and suggested a holiday. He concurred, and asked his superintendent for the necessary leave.

It was natural to think of England, 'the old country', where they both claimed roots. They asked Annie's mother to come and stay with the boys, arranged for a rented car to be at the airport, and landed at Heathrow in the rain in the second week in May. The idea was to travel, staying at places that offered bed and breakfast, in the south first, then on up to the Lake District.

Their first experience was in a two-star hotel in a resort on the coast of Dorset which they reached on the first night, groggy from jet-lag. There the landlord showed them a huge, dank bedroom with two double beds and two cots.

'It's a family room,' the owner said. A small pot-bellied man with an RAF moustache, cavalry twill trousers, and egg-stains on his checkered waistcoat. 'You can have it for the price of a double.'

'I only need one bed,' Salter said, looking around at the chipped paint on the floorboards, and glancing at the hand-written notices by the light switches, limiting the hours of enjoyment of everything from taking baths to eating in bed.

'I would normally put a family in here. Full board, four people,' the host said. 'Still.'

'How much?' Salter asked. Take your time, he thought, as he watched the man add up their 'American' accents, the pouring rain, and Annie's weariness as he arrived at his price.

'Twenty-six pounds,' the man said. 'That includes breakfast.'

'I know,' Salter said. He did a mental sum. 'Fifty dollars,' he said to Annie, who just shrugged. Salter looked around the room again. Perhaps, he thought, with one small extra effort we could find one of those hotels in the British Airways pamphlets, with Robert Morley as the host.

'If you take dinner, I could let you have it for twenty-one,' the host said, watching him.

'How much is dinner?'

'Nine pounds fifty. Inclusive, of course. Say forty pounds altogether.'

'Oh, Charlie, let's take it,' Annie said, sitting on the edge of one of the beds.

'Right you are, then,' the host said. 'No

22

need for a deposit, of course.' He moved to the door. 'I'll bring your bags up if you'll give me your keys. I think I know your car.'

While they were waiting, Annie tried each of the two double beds. One of them sloped heavily into a pit in the centre: the other one was oddly hard, and when Salter lifted the mattress, which seemed to be stuffed with old teddy-bears, he found the sagging frames of two single cots lashed together so that where they met an iron ridge ran down the centre of the bed. Salter moved to the window and watched his host in the parking lot below examine their baggage labels and peer into the glove compartment of their car. When he arrived with the bags at the bedroom door, he had one more message. He pointed to the notice on the door of the bathroom across the hall. 'We ask you not to take baths before dinner, or after ten o'clock or during the breakfast hours,' he said. 'Enjoy your stay.'

It went on like that. Dinner was a five course affair, if you counted the half grapefruit at the beginning and the triangle of processed cheese, still in its tinfoil, at the end. The soup was 'Potage Maison', a gelatinous suspension of bits of parsley. The entrée was a flat disc of grey meat, accompanied by serving dishes of carrots, potatoes, cabbage stalks and diced turnips, all served in small pools of the water they had been boiled in.

Picking their way wondrously through all this, the Salters drank a bottle of wine and ate some bread. 'Dessert,' Annie said, 'will be tapioca pudding and custard.' But she was wrong. Before Salter could ask her what tapioca was, they were served some crusts of bread soaked in milk in which some raisins were floating. 'What's this?' Salter asked, long past anger and despair, and now merely curious. 'Bread and butter pudding,' the waiter said.

Instant coffee was served in the sun lounge, a chilly glass-enclosed annexe furnished in broken rattan. 'It's probably quite nice here in hot weather,' Annie said, hugging herself against the chill. They had a drink in the empty bar and retired for the night, dirty, insufficiently fed, and cold. Then a turnaround occurred. As they crawled into the hollow bed ('It's just damp, not wet,' Annie assured him), Annie started to giggle, and Salter, picking up her mood, expanded it into some horseplay which brushed aside their new diffidence and turned into a happy, uncomplicated tumble that dissolved most of their problems of the last three months. They were so cheerful in the morning that not even the single cold fried egg they were served for breakfast, or the additional charge for VAT ('only the dinner was inclusive, sir') could upset them, and they drove off early in the rain in case some redeeming feature should spoil the squalor of their first night in England.

'What are we going to do?' Salter asked.

'We are going to be very, very careful,' Annie said. 'We will start looking for a place to stay at three in the afternoon, and we are going to buy some guidebooks.'

They drove along the coast road to Torbay through the lush green countryside while Annie, an avid gardener, exclaimed steadily at the profligacy of the English spring. 'They pack so much in,' she said. 'They must spend all their time gardening.'

'When it's not raining,' Salter said. He was having to concentrate hard to follow the road through the mist. In Torbay they bought every guide to good food and accommodation they could find, and spent an hour in a pub matching up recommendations. They settled for their second night on an inn on the other coast near Clovelly, telephoned to make a reservation, and headed inland, exchanging primrose-filled lanes for lonely, gloom-haunted moorlands. Salter detoured slightly in order to have a look at the prison, but the thickening mist soon sent him scurrying back to the main road before they could come within sight of it. All afternoon they picked their way across the peninsula, concentrating on not getting lost.

They had decided to take up their reservation only if the place looked inviting, and at five o'clock they approached it warily. Salter pulled up on the highway, a few yards short of the inn.

'The grass is cut,' Annie said. The experience of the night before might have been avoided if they had paid careful attention to the signs of decay on the outside of the hotel.

'Flowers are nice,' Salter said, pointing to a bed of gillyflowers in the centre of the grass. They got out of the car and walked forward.

'Smells good,' Annie said, putting her head in the door. They ought to have noticed the smell of cabbage yesterday. 'Let's do it,' she said.

A pleasant-looking woman in young middle-age was behind the desk, and Salter asked for a double room. The woman laid a card in front of him which listed the amenities of the hotel, and the precise charges, which were nearly identical to those they had paid the night before.

But nothing else was the same. The room, part of a new extension tucked in behind the hotel, was warm, well-furnished, and cunningly fitted with everything they looked for, including a television set concealed in a cupboard which could be switched on and off from the bed. When they asked where the bathroom was and if it would be all right to have a bath, the woman looked surprised and opened the door to an adjoining bathroom which a Swiss hotelier would have admired. The water was boiling.

Dinner began with game pâté, followed by roast lamb so tender they had to gobble it before it melted, and a choice of desserts from which they selected one made with grapes and sour cream which had Annie nearly crying with pleasure. Again coffee was served in the lounge, but this time the lounge was a small library full of armchairs, with a fire blazing in the hearth.

There was one other resident, a middle-aged man pouring himself coffee who, as they sat down, offered to pour some for them. A gent with a private income who lives here year-round on his income from his rubber plantation, thought Salter, noting the expensive thorn-proof clothes, the manicured hands, the handkerchief up the sleeve, and the mild, weathered look, probably acquired hunting and fishing.

'On holiday?' the man inquired.

'Yes,' Salter said. 'You?'

The man shook his head. 'I don't work, so I'm never on holiday,' he said. 'I live here during this part of the year. You are Canadian?'

'Yes. Is it that obvious?'

'If you know the signs. Canadians have none of the American brashness or the English preoccupation with class and manners which would have had you circling the room for five minutes before you decided you wanted to be spoken to by me.'

'A perfect blend of the best of both?' Annie asked. 'Lovely us?'

'On the other hand, though, some of you combine the unattractive national characteristics of both. Canadians, in short, can be positive mongrels or negative ones.'

Christ, thought Salter, we've only been here three minutes. But Annie took to eccentric situations like Alice.

'You've thought about this a lot?' she asked.

'That's what I do, dear lady. I have lots of time.'

'My husband only said two words,' Annie said. 'We might have been Australians. How did you know we weren't, just by looking at us?'

'Because the landlady told me.' He uncrossed his legs and leaned forward with a little giggle. 'I don't think I can keep this rubbish up any more,' he said. 'Let's have a drink and you tell me what you've seen so far.'

Annie laughed. Salter, who had been nearly taken in, was relieved to find it was a little game, and he launched into an account of the differences between the two identically priced hotels they had stayed at so far. The brandy arrived while he was talking, and the man's face began to take on the charged air of a television set warming up. When Salter finished, he was ready.

'Now *that*,' he said, 'is something I can tell

you about. What you've stumbled on is the English pairing system. You'll find it works throughout the service industry here.' He rose an inch in his chair with the joy of a really good story to tell. 'Everybody who has to deal with the public in this country has a double,' he began. 'I'll call them Tweedledum and Tweedledee. Now Tweedledum is entirely benevolent — friendly, courteous, eager to serve — thoroughly wonderful in all the ways his job allows. Tweedledee, on the other hand, if your wife will pardon me, is a prize pig. As Tweedledum enjoys serving people, so, conversely, Tweedledee gets his pleasure from being surly, swindling and bloody-minded. No, no, let me go on. I am convinced that Tweedledum and Tweedledee are aware of each other, *know* each other, actually pair up, so that at some hoteliers' conference in the past, the owners of this hostel met the owners of your last night's horror show and they decided which would be which. Hang on a minute. It works, in my experience, everywhere — bus-drivers, policemen — struck a chord, have I? — shop assistants — every Tweedledum has a Tweedledee. And they *know* each other. Further, I have found out that they sometimes switch roles. Not long ago, I was in a ticket queue at Waterloo station and became aware as my queue shuffled forward that we had a grade one pig behind the window. He was sneering at old ladies, contemptuous of foreigners – generally performing his role to the hilt. Now at the other window – yes, another brandy would be nice – was a real Sunny Jim. Couldn't be more helpful; suggesting cheaper ways of travelling, telling people the best part of the train to get on for their purpose, cheerfully changing fifty-pound notes. Tweedledum and Tweedledee. Don't interrupt. I'm nearly there. Now, a very strange thing happened. As I approached the window, very nervous because I had several questions I wanted to ask, the two ticket sellers went to the back of the room and had a little conversation. When they returned to their cages, my man smiled at me and asked me what he could do for me. He was positively servile as we worked our way through my problems. At the same time, I could hear the seller in the next window – the former nice chap, you remember – shouting at a child for daring to try to pay for her ticket with a handful of tenpenny pieces, as snotty as a French museum attendant. You see? I

31

am convinced that they were dum-ing and dee-ing in shifts, one hour as Tweedledum and one hour as Tweedledee. Now, here is my worry. I am terrified that this place will end its Tweedledum period any day now and we shall all be faced at dinner with Brown Windsor Soup and frozen cod and Brussels sprouts, with prunes and custard for pudding.' The man finished his brandy with a flourish and stood up.

'That,' Salter said, 'is the most terrific load of balls I've ever heard in my life.'

'All true, though,' the man said. 'All true. You'll see.' He left the room in triumph.

Salter looked at Annie. 'You think there's anything in it?' he asked.

'It accounts for the facts, which is what matters. Now let's go to bed before someone ordinary comes along.'

For the next four days they steered their way through the minefield of English hospitality, never finding anything as bad as their first night or as good as their second, until they came by accident, to Boomewood, which had all the markings of a genuine Tweedledum.

A knock at the door was followed by a voice saying that dinner would be ready in ten minutes. Salter woke up Annie, and they presented themselves in the dining-room which was already nearly full. An excessively handsome, dark-haired waiter took them to a table set for two and said, 'Dinner?'

'Could we see a menu?' Annie asked.

'No menu,' the waiter said. 'Dinner?'

A woman at the next table leaned over. 'Trust them,' she said, from behind very thick glasses. The man with her nodded.

The soup was delicious and it was followed by cross-sections of a calf's leg, accompanied by slightly sticky yellow rice.

'*Osso buco*,' Bottle Glasses said. 'Veal shanks. And risotto.'

The Salters tucked in happily. The dessert was a water-ice. 'Yum yum,' Annie said happily.

Once more they were invited to take coffee in the residents' lounge, which they assumed would be packed like the dining-room, but only the lady in the thick glasses and her husband followed them in. The coffee was espresso.

'Want to know what you've stumbled into?' their new companion asked when they were seated with their coffee. 'This is the best food, for the price, in the Midlands, if you like Florentine cooking.' She flashed her lenses at them. 'They only serve one menu – it's pot luck, but by God, what a pot. Last night they had *spaghetti carbonara* and veal kidneys cooked in Marsala. I thought my husband was going to faint, didn't I, Henry?'

Henry nodded. 'That's right,' he said.

'And a chocolate thing for dessert that made the backs of my knees damp as it went down. Didn't it, Henry?'

'That's right,' Henry said, and made as if to speak again.

She cut him off. 'Breakfast is a giant cup of *caffè latte* and fresh rolls if you like. If you want sausages and fried bread you should leave tonight and good riddance to you.'

Salter wondered if he was going to spend the evenings of the next three weeks being entertained by garrulous eccentrics in residents' lounges. It was not an unpleasant prospect.

'Where is everybody?' he asked, more to keep Bottle Glasses going than because he cared. From the nose down, she was an attractive woman, about forty, in a dark red woollen dress and matching shoes, with jaunty breasts and thin, muscular legs. Only the glasses and the difficulty of making eye contact with her made the initial social

34

skirmishing awkward.

'There are very few guests at the moment,' she said. 'Just us and an American girl. Oh, and a Canadian woman, a Miss Rundstedt, at least I think she's Canadian. I've been trying to find out. All the rest are local people, attracted by the food. They don't take reservations for the dining-room, so every night there's a line-up outside the door at seven. First come, first served. Only one sitting.'

'Have you been staying here long?' Annie asked.

'A week. We stumbled on it last year, like you, and we came back this year just to eat for a couple of weeks after a winter of the *haute cuisine* at Watford, where we live. You're not English, are you?'

'No.'

'American?'

'No.

'I didn't think so.'

There was a pause.

'We're Canadian.'

'Ah. Well, that's a bit of a conversation stopper, isn't it? But let me tell you about this place. It's run by a man about whom I have my doubts, don't I, Henry? He has a very curious accent, which he believes is upper, but is really the sort of accent that ships' pursers and masters of ceremonies at holiday camps have: very put-on, but I can't be sure what he's putting off. He may be Australian. His wife, whom you met (I was in the lounge here when you arrived), is Italian, and her brother speaks no English and waited at table tonight.'

Nobody said anything for a few moments. Then: 'Haven't you been able to find out more than that?' Salter asked.

'Your husband is being ironical,' the woman said to Annie. 'But I don't mind. I'm a very nosey woman; it's my chief pleasure in life. Isn't it, Henry?'

'What are your other pleasures?' Annie asked. 'By the way, would you like to know who we are?' She introduced them to the other couple.

'I'm Maud Beresford,' the woman said. 'And this is my husband, Henry. Henry's a doctor, aren't you, Henry, but he spends all his time in a laboratory playing with rats.'

'I'm a psychologist,' Henry said.

'He's summing you up right now,' Maud said. 'But he never lets on what he knows. Not like me.'

Henry lit a pipe. He was dressed for survival in a thick pair of trousers, a tweed jacket over a hairy pullover, a khaki shirt, a woollen Paisley tie, and shoes with leather laces and double soles. 'I'm on holiday, dear,' he said, pinching out sparks as they landed on his trousers. 'Besides, I'm interested in typical behaviour. I'm not a psychiatrist.'

'And what do you do?' Maud asked Salter, cutting Henry off.

'I'm a maintenance supervisor for the Toronto Transit Commission,' he said. 'The bus company,' he explained.

'I don't believe a word of it. What about you, Annie?'

'Me? I'm a housewife.'

Maud looked at them both in turn. 'I suspect you are both running away from your respective spouses,' she said. 'Never mind. If you stay here for two days I'll find out all about you. Come along, Henry. Let's go to bed. It's been a dreary day except for the *osso buco* and the mysterious Salters. See you at breakfast.'

Henry winked and followed her out.

'What do you think?' Salter asked when the door had closed. 'Shall we check out now

37

or wait until the morning?'

'Why, Charlie? I enjoyed them, didn't you?'

'Oh, sure. But it will only take her about five minutes to blow my cover. Then she'll tell everyone else.'

'You'd better practise getting your story straight, hadn't you? Make a change for you, being on the other side.' She laughed. 'I feel very cheered up, so let's go to bed.'

The day seemed to deserve a nightcap which they drank as they were getting undressed. The conversation with Maud had left Salter in an absurd mood, and when he finished his drink, he took off his clothes and stood over Annie who was already under the covers.

'Nancy,' he said in what he imagined was the voice of his favourite fictional character, Bill Sikes, as played by Robert Newton, 'Nancy, I wants yer body.'

'Shshsh,' Annie said.

Salter, surprised, stopped dead. Annie pointed to the window, where the curtain was drawn tight, and put a finger to her lips.

'Nancy,' Salter growled again. 'I'm a-coming for yer,' then stopped again as he heard it, a giggle from outside. They were being overheard. He started to speak again, but this time he moved towards the window as he spoke. 'You've been avoiding me all day, Nancy,' he said, 'and I'm claiming me rights, see. You know what I like before I go out on a burgle, so let's 'ave yer.' He jumped for the window and pulled back the curtain in time to see a shadow disappear around the corner of the house. 'Christ,' he said. 'A genuine Peeping Tom. I'd better tell the landlord. Tomorrow.' He closed the curtains and made sure the door was locked, and came back to the bed in his own character. 'Do you think it might be Maud?' he asked as he gathered Annie to him.

In the morning it turned out that Maud had exaggerated slightly. There was indeed *caffè latte* for breakfast, but there was bacon and eggs, too, and Salter ordered some of everything. The Beresfords joined them at a table for four, and Maud resumed her inquiries.

'Do maintenance supervisors for the bus company get four weeks' holiday every year?' she asked, when she had cleared the ground with a few preliminary questions.

'We save them up,' Salter said. 'You can

39

add your overtime to your regular vacation allowance.'

Maud's eyes travelled lightly over Annie, pricing her shoes and her jewellery. 'Hmmmm,' she said. 'What are your plans for today? Not moving on immediately, I hope?'

It was something they had talked about in the bedroom that morning. For nearly a week now they had been locked in the car in the rain, and Annie wanted to stop. The skies were still slate-coloured, but no rain was actually falling, and she suggested that they take advantage of their luck and stay at Boomewood for a few days, exploring the countryside in daily outings. Salter was agreeable. Now that they were in England, Annie, who had done her homework, had a lot of gardens, houses and castles she wanted to see. But Salter did not know what he wanted to do. Or rather, he did know; he wanted to do nothing, hang about the pubs and live the life, chatting up the natives while Annie went sightseeing. In a nutshell, he wanted to wander around Soho while Annie visited the Royal Academy. So long as it was raining there was no conflict, but now Annie was dusting off her guide-books again.

When they took possession of their new car, she had plans.

Annie said, 'If they have room, I think we'll be staying here for a while.'

'Good,' Maud said. 'What are your plans for today?'

They explained about the car, and Annie mentioned her desire to see some famous gardens in the neighbourhood.

'Why don't you let us take you?' Maud cried. 'Let *him* worry about the car.' She pointed to Salter. 'We want to see the gardens, too, but we need a guide, don't we, Henry? Do you know anything about flowers? I just know daffodils and geraniums, but I love smelling them. Henry does, too. Let's the three of us go and leave the maintenance supervisor to haggle with the garage.'

Salter and Annie exchanged three or four glances and conveyed between them that it sounded like a good plan, and that Maud, at least, was an entertaining companion in spite of or including her compulsive nosiness, so they agreed. The Beresfords would drop Salter off, and the other three would go on to the gardens. They would return to Boomewood sometime during the afternoon and Salter could do what he liked, including

41

following them if the car had arrived. It was perfect. Tokesbury Mallett looked just big enough for a couple of hours' walkabout, and that plus a pub lunch would do him nicely.

They were interrupted by the approach of the waiter, a fair youth of about seventeen.

'Ah,' Maud said. ' "The Smarmy Boy." '

'Here we are, then, ladies and gentlemen. I *am* sorry to keep you waiting. Bacon and eggs for you, sir, careful with the plate, it's very hot. *Caffè latte* all round. Don't spill any on your nice suit, ma'am; and rolls, nice and hot. Butter. Oh, I'm sorry, I'll be back in a jiffy. Here, I'll give you the butter on this table. Anything else, anybody? Marmalade? Jam? Ketchup, sir? I know you Americans like it on most things. Worcester sauce, sir? No? I'll leave you to it, then. Just call out, won't you. I'm in the kitchen.'

It was Uriah Heep being played against type by Michael York: a handsome youth from whom unctuousness in a local accent oozed like treacle.

'Who is that?' Annie asked Maud automatically.

'Gregory,' Maud said. 'Gregory is an apprentice electrician who lives in a room over the garage and pays for his keep by helping out with odd jobs, including waiting at table, when electrical work is slow. Our landlady took pity on him when his mother went off somewhere a year ago, probably to shake off Gregory. Only a foreigner would not see that such ingratiating manners in an English youth today are not normal.'

'Probably a Tweedledum who has over-balanced backwards,' Annie said.

'A what?'

Annie explained.

'What a lovely theory. Quite true, too. Isn't it, Henry?'

Henry, who had been trying surreptitiously to read the paper, looked up. 'I told you dear, Gregory is probably an extreme case of Wanker's Self-Doubt,' Henry said.

'What?' asked Annie and Salter.

Maud for the first time looked discomposed. 'Henry retreats into psychological jargon sometimes,' she said, 'Ah, look. Our American friend.'

The girl who seated herself at a table for one would have looked at home on any American campus during the last twenty-five years: black turtleneck sweater, kilt-type skirt, black woollen stockings and penny loafers – almost the same costume as that

43

worn by the first girl Salter had wooed during his brief college career. They watched her dispose of Gregory's attempt to get her to smile at him while ordering her breakfast.

'She's in love with Mario,' Maud said. 'Last night's waiter. He gets his pick of the girls, I would think. And now here comes Miss Rundstedt, your compatriot.'

A woman of about forty entered the room with the delicate steps of a young girl. She had a tiny face topped with frizzy red hair which fanned out from the top of her head at a forty-five-degree angle, in an Egyptian style. She had very large breasts which she rested on her arms while she talked to Gregory.

'A bit mysterious, like you,' Maud said. 'On holiday, apparently, but I've seen her about town on very friendly terms with mysterious strangers in pubs.'

'But not with you, dear,' Henry said.

'No,' Maud agreed. 'I'd say she dodges me.'

'That it, then?' Salter asked. 'Can we go now?'

While they separated to pick up raincoats and cameras, Salter went in search of the host. He found him in a dark little office

44

at the end of the downstairs hallway, a man in his late fifties with a large grey beard and hornrimmed glasses, wearing a heavily striped shirt and a club tie under a woollen cardigan.

'Everything satisfactory, sir?' he asked, when Salter had introduced himself.

'Perfect,' Salter said and went on to explain the purpose of his visit.

'Peeping Tom, eh? We've never had a complaint like that before. Couldn't have been mistaken, sir?'

'No,' Salter said, registering the man's lie. An automatic defence of the establishment's virtue?

'We'll keep an eye open, then,' the host said and waited for Salter to go.

'Would you like me to mention it to the police at Tokesbury?' Salter suggested. 'I'm calling in on the inspector this morning.'

'No need, no need. Leave it to me. You have official business with the police, do you, sir?'

'No, I don't,' Salter said, surprised at the directness of the question. He explained about the accident.

'Yes, of course. Maria told me. Rotten luck, that. Never mind. Insured, of course?'

45

Salter nodded.

'Good,' the man said, and turned back to his desk.

Salter was mildly intrigued by his landlord, who seemed to prefer this cave at the end of the hall to the hotel's public rooms. His manner to Salter was polite, but not expansive: there was not enough ebullience there to run a successful bar. But if you've got an attractive Italian wife, twenty years younger than yourself, you can leave her to keep the public happy, thought Salter. Especially if she can cook like that.

The rest of the party was assembled in the hall and they drove Salter into the town and left him outside the police station, where Inspector Churcher was waiting for him in his immaculately tidy office, looking himself as if he had attended to the items of his personal appearance with a check-list.

'I was waiting for you to join me for coffee, Inspector,' Churcher said. 'You will have some, I hope?' When Salter nodded, Churcher asked, 'White or black?'

Coffee-coloured, thought Salter, wondering which of the dozen varieties of drink the English called coffee he was going to get.

'White,' he said aloud in case it came out of a bottle.

Churcher called the request through the doorway and Sergeant Robey brought in two cups of a milky grey liquid.

Churcher shot his cuffs and started in.

'You play golf?' he asked.

'No,' Salter lied instinctively.

'Pity,' Churcher said. 'I didn't before I came here, but I think that community relations are very important, so I've joined the local golf and tennis clubs. Quite enjoy it, too. I've been urging my men to get involved. Not at golf, of course, but at their own level.'

What would that be — skittles for constables, lawn-bowling for sergeants? 'Don't they live here?' Salter asked.

'Ah yes, I take your point,' Churcher said. 'But I think they could easily become detached, once they join the Force. Don't you agree? What sort of activities do your people encourage?'

'Various things, Inspector. Boxing clubs, that kind of thing. And we are putting more men back on the beat.'

'Very wise. By the way, my name is Charles. Charles Churcher. C.C. My father wanted a carbon copy of himself.' He chuckled and looked invitingly at Salter.

After a struggle, Salter said, 'Charlie.'

Churcher's mouth opened into a huge smile. 'Really,' he said. 'Really. How extraordinary. Tell me, Charles, do your men get any special training in crowd control. I was just looking at a report on the French methods. Very interesting.'

Salter looked through the window at two old men rioting on the bench by the bus-stop. There was no one else in sight. How long does a little chat go on, he wondered. 'It's part of our general training,' he said. And then: 'By the way, there's a Peeping Tom at Boomewood.' He told Churcher the story of the previous night.

'The Prowler, eh? Sergeant!' he called. When the sergeant of the night before appeared, Churcher said, 'Come in. Close the door. Now, Charles, I'd like you to repeat your story if you would. Just as you told it to me.'

Jesus Christ, thought Salter, but he did as he was asked.

'Now. What do you think, Sergeant?' Churcher said, as if he were giving the sergeant a little test.

'I think someone was listening outside the inspector's window,' the sergeant said, after consideration.

'Surely more than *that*, Sergeant. This is the second incident, remember.'

'They may not be connected, sir. One is listening, as the inspector tells it, and the other is tickling feet, saying "wakey-wakey". They might be quite different types of people.' The sergeant said this with the air of a man exposing a serious flaw in a complex theory.

He's going too far, thought Salter, as he watched to see if Churcher would react to this tiny pull on his leg.

'Of course, they both seem to have a common basis in sexual motivation, sir,' the sergeant offered.

Churcher brushed away any doubts. 'I think they *must* be connected, Sergeant. Look into it, will you?'

'Right, sir,' the sergeant said, his glance barely touching Salter as he made his exit.

Salter stood up. 'Thanks for the coffee,' he said. 'Now I think I'll go for a stroll around town.'

'Would you like a guide, Charles?' Churcher offered.

'No, thanks. If you are known in the community, they might wonder who I am,' Salter said. Especially if Maud sees us. 'I'm still a maintenance supervisor for the Toronto bus company, on holiday.'

'Of course. I understand. Well, drop in again, won't you. I enjoyed our little talk.' Churcher put out his hand, and Salter left.

He was joined on the steps of the station house by Sergeant Robey. 'We have our share of Peeping Tom reports,' the sergeant said. 'But I'll tell the boys to keep a watch out.'

'Have fun, Sergeant. What do you know about the staff at Boomewood?' he asked.

'Why, sir? Something fishy about them?'

'No, no. But it's an unusual place to find in the middle of England. Who's the owner? Where's he from?'

'Somewhere in the south, sir. London way, I should think. We did a bit of homework on him after the prowler incident. He came into the district two years ago and bought Boomewood, which was a dump at the time, and, well, you can see what he's done with it. He opened up at the end of the season and last year was his first full year. He's a bit of an odd one. No record or nothing. He met his wife in Italy, apparently, and brought her back here. The waiter is her brother. Came over on a work permit a couple of months ago to learn English. That's it, except for Mrs Peabody, their daily, and that kid Gregory. They must work hard.'

'They do,' Salter said. 'It's paying off, too. Now, Sergeant. Point me to that pub you mentioned yesterday.'

'The Eagle and Child, sir? Down there, first turning on the left, sir. Try their ham. He cures it himself.'

'Okay. Now what else should I see around here?'

'Well, sir, there's Broodleigh Castle which was built by one of James the First's favourites,' the Sergeant began.

Salter cut him off. 'I was thinking of something a bit livelier,' he said. 'Like a sheep-shearing contest.'

'If you stay till Saturday there's the annual shin-kicking contest over at Chipping Camden, sir. A bit of a drive, but very nice when the sun's out.'

'That sounds more like it,' Salter said. 'But what about today?'

'If I were off-duty, I'd be at the races,' the sergeant said, looking nowhere in particular.

'That's it. Where?'

'Right here, sir. About two miles down that road. We have a little meeting three times a year. Over the sticks.'

'Sticks?'

'Fences, sir. Steeplechasing.'

'Just my meat. What time?'

'I believe the first race is at two o'clock. If you do go, try a few bob on Joe's Folly in the third. Napper Marston trains him. He's a local lad we've taken an interest in once or twice. He mentioned yesterday they were having a go with this one.'

'Joe's Folly. Right. Thanks.'

'Good luck, sir. Might win your holiday money, eh, sir?'

Salter set off in the direction of the Eagle and Child, and then, since it was still only eleven-thirty, took a wide detour to look at the market street. He stopped at a street trader, attracted by a beautiful display of polished apples, and asked for a pound, pointing to the ones he wanted. The assistant turned his back and picked out three from under his feet and weighed them up, swung the bag expertly tight, and offered it to Salter.

'I want those three,' Salter said, pointing

to the display. A little queue was forming behind him.

'Can't pick and choose, guv. Take the rough with the smooth,' the assistant said. ' 'Ere. Forty pee.'

'Sure I can. I want those,' Salter insisted. Behind him the queue started mumbling.

' 'Oo does he think he is?' one woman said.

'I don't know about that,' replied a huge, black-haired woman in a pinafore and carpet-slippers. 'Time somebody said somethink.'

'You want them or not, squire?' the assistant demanded.

'No,' Salter said.

'Right. Next!' The assistant emptied the bag into the container at his feet. 'Bleedin' Americans,' he said.

Salter moved a few yards down the street to another barrow. 'I'd like those three apples,' he said loudly. '*Those* three.'

'Certainly, guv, which ones? That one and that one and *that* one? Right. Forty-eight pee, please. Cheers. Now then, darlin', what can I do for you?'

Salter went on his way, wondering.

The Eagle and Child served a good lunch of

ham rolls and pickles, and he found a place at the bar and tucked in.

' 'On holiday, sir?' the barman asked.

Salter nodded.

'Staying in the area?'

They really are a nosey lot, thought Salter. It's just that Maud is more honest. He nodded again.

'At the Swan, I presume?'

'No. At Boomewood, as a matter of fact.'

Two yards along the counter, a man in a hacking jacket with a bushy moustache caught his attention. 'Like it?' he asked. 'Boomewood, I mean. Thought I might try it myself. I hear it's pretty good.'

'It's good,' Salter said. 'I'd recommend it.'

The man nodded. 'Just touring, are you? From Canada?'

'Yes,' Salter said, faintly irritated. Did he smell of maple syrup? 'How did you know?' he asked.

'I lived there for a bit.'

'Oh? Whereabouts?'

'Here and there. Where are you from?'

'Toronto. I work for the bus company.'

'I spent most of my time in Winnipeg. Do you know it?'

'I've been there. A long time ago. I don't know it now.'

'It hasn't changed much. Not like Toronto. What do you have on the agenda today? Stately homes?'

'No. I'm going to the races.'

'Oh, really? I'm going there myself. You follow racing here?'

'I've never been to a steeplechase in my life. The only racing I know anything about is harness-racing.'

'Greenwood, eh?' The man smiled companionably. 'Like some company? I'll show you the ropes.'

While they were talking, Salter had been trying to get a fix on his companion. He had taken in the man's brand-new clothes and watched him pay for a drink with a healthy wad of bills which he kept in a money clip. There was a smell of sharpness about the man; a hint of the con man brushed the policeman's antennae. Would he try to set Salter up? Introduce him to three friends and a pack of cards? Salter was intrigued.

'All right,' he said. 'When do we leave? I'll see if my car's ready.' He explained what had happened to him.

'Leave it here. We'll go in mine. Finish

your beer and we'll be off.'

And so it was arranged. Twenty minutes later they were in a light stream of traffic heading towards the racecourse.

'My name's Parrott. Jeremy Parrott,' the man said when they were under way.

'Charlie Salter. What did you do in Winnipeg?'

'Worked for the government. Public works. I supervised government building contracts.'

'Are you retired now?' The man was in his early fifties.

'Temporarily. The NDP got back into power and they put their own people in. Spoils of office. But they won't last.'

It was a familiar story in Canadian politics. Salter's background in the working class district of Cabbagetown in Toronto had made him incapable of supporting either of the major parties had he been able to distinguish between them, at the same time as he recognized the possible truth in the assumption of the worldly-wise that the New Democratic Party had kept its virtue intact because no one had yet offered anything for it. Nevertheless, he remained a closet socialist until such time as an honest man

56

appeared elsewhere. His new companion had just revealed his affiliation with the Conservatives, so Salter shut up.

The stream of traffic turned down a narrow lane, through what looked like a space in a hedge, into a field. Some of the cars parked here, but Parrott drove across the field to a gap in a rail fence which turned out to be the track itself. Here an attendant took some money from them and waved them across the track. They drove on to the centre of the course and turned to park by one of the brushwood fences the horses had to jump.

'This is the public enclosure,' Parrott said. 'We'll watch most of it from those stands over there, but I like to watch one right by the fence. I like to see them jump. If we park here we can sit in the car if it rains, and be ready to take off after the last race. Now let me show you round.'

They walked down the course to where a small crowd was gathered around some book-makers who were beginning to call the odds. Salter was stunned by the squalor. His only experience of racing in Toronto, where even the cheapest seats are under cover and only the horses brave the elements, had not prepared him for this. The public enclosure was an open field, now a swamp, in the centre of which stood a ramshackle wooden shed with a corrugated iron roof. Inside this hut a small crowd was drinking tea and beer. By the rail a dozen bookmakers were gathered under huge umbrellas. Everyone else stood in the open, soaking up the rain.

His companion explained what was happening, and Salter decided to bet. He picked a horse at random and walked up to the nearest bookmaker, a small cheerful-looking man whose board proclaimed that he was Jack Edwards from Nottingham, 50p Minimum, E.W. taken.

'I'd like to place a bet of two pounds to win on Mitcham Lane in the first race,' Salter said.

'And so you shall, my old darlin',' Jack Edwards said. He took a printed card from a pack he was holding and spoke to the ancient tramp beside him who was holding a ledger. 'The gentleman wishes to wager two sovereigns on Mitcham Lane in the first race, Frederick.' He said, 'Shall we accept his offer at odds of seven to two?'

The nearby bookies laughed. Salter took the card from the grinning Edwards and stepped back to see why he had made a fool of himself.

'Just say "Two pounds, Mitcham Lane,"' his companion suggested. 'It's easier.'

Mitcham Lane fell over half way round the course, out of sight of the public enclosure, and Salter threw away his ticket. They had agreed to cross the track for most of the races, to watch them from the stands, but before they reached the rail, there was a commotion down the track where two men in red coats on horseback were surrounded by a pack of dogs. Then the voice of the Queen came over the loudspeakers.

'Good afternoon, everyone,' the Queen said. 'Welcome to the third meeting of the season, sponsored today by your local Hunt. My name is Alison Lamprey and I am secretary of the Tokesbury Mallett pack. I won't detain you for more than a moment, but we are here to make an appeal to you, the local sportsmen, who love horses and for whom National Hunt Racing is so important. We of the Tokesbury Mallett Hunt ask you to support us in resisting the efforts of some outside groups who are trying to interfere with the traditional English sport of hunting. I won't bore you with the reasons why hunting is *not* a cruel sport, and *not* in any way harmful to the agricultural interests among you— you know all that— but I would just like to say to you that hunting is the backbone, the lifeblood, of the sport you are gathered here today to enjoy. Without us, without hunting, there would be very few horses for steeplechasing and the sport would very quickly die. So, please, write to your local newspaper, and to the national papers, to show your support for us. And now we thought that you would like to see some of the colour and drama of a hunt in full chase so we have brought you the Tokesbury pack, who will run down the course, accompanied by Mr Simnel and Viscount Oates, the joint masters of the hunt. When you are ready, gentlemen?'

There was the sound of a horn, and down the course came the dogs, followed by the two riders in red coats. When the pack was opposite the crowd, one of the riders turned his head sideways and made a sound like a coyote barking. When the pack reached the end of the course, they turned and ran back, and this time the rider howled into the stands.

'Thank you all,' said the Queen.

Salter looked around at the crowd, expecting cheers, or hoots of derision, but there was nothing. A small silence was broken by Jack Edwards, shouting, 'Right, lads. 'Oo wants a bet? Come on, support your local bloodsport. Seven to one, bar one.' Otherwise the event had caused no more commotion or interest than a low-flying aeroplane.

'You think that'll help?' he asked Parrott.

'Can you see this lot writing to *The Times?*' Parrott replied.

'Do they *believe* it?'

'They didn't even hear it. They came here to bet.'

'So did I.'

They paid some more money to cross the course and enter a large shed where the well-heeled patrons were keeping dry. From here he had the satisfaction of seeing his choice in the next race unseat his rider and gallop off down the course alone.

'I've got a tip on the next one,' Salter said, and told his companion what it was.

'It's ten to one,' Parrott noted. 'I should get on now if I were you.'

'Fiver. Joe's Folly,' Salter said to the bookmaker out of the corner of his mouth.

Before the race began, the odds had

shortened to six to one.

'They've come for it,' Parrott said.

The horse was ridden by the trainer's son. When the starter's flag went down, it set off at a fast gallop and by the end of two miles it was three furlongs clear. Salter's money was as good as in the bank. Then the others set off in pursuit and started to close the gap. With two furlongs left, Joe's Folly was still fifty yards in front, but staggering badly. Behind it, four fresher-looking horses were making a grim charge. Joe's Folly cleared three more fences and there was one left, but by now the horse was weaving from side to side. The four other horses swept by it and rushed for the last fence, and then, just as Salter got ready to throw his ticket away, the leader stumbled and fell as he landed over the last fence, bringing down two of his companions. Joe's Folly chose a broken spot in the fence to crawl through behind the only other horse, who looked certain to win now, but as the crowd roared them home, the rider on the leading horse began to slip sideways. He clung desperately to the neck of his horse for a few yards, but the horse shook him off and Joe's Folly tottered alone past the winning post.

'Well done,' Parrott said. 'I wouldn't back him again, though.'

A man on Salter's other side spoke. 'It oughta be stopped,' he cried. 'Puttin' bleedin' cripples on good 'orses. Did you see him? Couldn't even stay on the bleeder at a canter. Gawd bloody 'ell. What won it? Bleeding Joe's Folly. A fucking fiddle. 'Oo'd back that thing?' He was beside himself with rage.

'I did,' Salter said.

'*You* did? *You* did? 'Ere, Alf.' He turned away from Salter. 'Bloke 'ere says he backed that sodding 'orse. Backed it to win!' He glared at Salter, then turned back to Alf. 'Come on. Let's go and 'ave a cuppa tea,' he said in disgust.

A few minutes later when Salter and Parrott entered the refreshment shed in search of a drink, he heard the man's voice behind him from a corner of the room.

'That's 'im, Alf. That's the bleeder 'oo backed that soddin' 'orse.'

Salter stayed in the tea line with his back to the voice, listening hard.

'That's 'im all right,' the voice continued. 'There.'

Another voice spoke. Alf. 'You know what,

63

Des,' the voice said, 'I bet he didn't do it at all. I think he was just trying to upset you.' And Alf laughed.

Salter won no more races. As promised, they watched the last race from the rail by the first fence, and Salter got a worm's eye view of three tons of horses as they rose into the air and smashed down on the other side. Watching the previous races from the insulating distance of the stands had not prepared him for the assault on his senses that this close-up provided. The horses themselves were an astonishing and beautiful sight (the nearest one was only six feet away), huge masses of shifting muscle sailing through the air, but the most vivid impression was of the enormous risks the jockeys took at each fence as they shouted from high in the air at their horses and each other, fighting for a safe and advantageous landing. To Salter, it looked like the most exciting and dangerous sport he had ever seen and he thought later, when he had gathered his senses together, that he would have liked, just once, to ride the safest horse in the world over one little fence just to see what it was like, even though he had never been on a horse in his life.

Walking to the car, he said, 'And one of them was a *girl!*' He was still, in spirit, by the fence.

'What?' Parrot asked. 'Oh, the jockeys. Yes. Women have been riding for a few years, I think. Going to try your luck tomorrow, or will you be moving on?'

Salter looked around and found himself on a racecourse. 'We are staying here for a few days. I'll be back tomorrow, all right. What about you?'

'I don't make any plans,' Parrot said. 'I might see you here. Depends.' Twenty minutes later he pulled up at the garage where Salter was to collect his car.

'Thanks,' Salter said, still in a slight daze. 'I enjoyed that.'

'Cheers,' Parrott said, and drove off.

Back at Boomewood Annie was having a bath after a happy day of sniffing flowers. Maud Beresford had suggested another expedition for the following day which Annie was keen to go on, and Salter saw his opportunity. He described his day at the races as enjoyable enough, carefully keeping back too much enthusiasm.

Annie said, 'Do you want to do something

else tomorrow? I don't have to go with Maud.'

'No, no,' he protested. 'You go. I'll amuse myself around here.'

Annie said, 'You could go to the races again tomorrow, couldn't you?'

'I might, yes. Yes, maybe I'll do that.'

'Good,' she said. 'Ask Henry. He looked a bit bored today.'

'All right.'

'Got what you wanted, Charlie? Good. So have I.' She turned on the hand shower to wash her hair. Salter reached over her back and turned the cold water tap on to full and left her yelping.

When she emerged he was sorting out his pockets and disposing of his betting tickets.

'We'll need some money tomorrow, Charlie,' she said. 'You'd better cash a traveller's cheque at the desk here.'

Salter reached into the wardrobe to find the spare jacket where he kept his passport and traveller's cheques. He took out the cheques, and paused. 'My passport's gone,' he said.

Annie moved over to him and patted the pockets of the jacket, reached inside and drew out the passport.

66

'It's in the wrong pocket,' he said.

He explained. The left-hand inside pocket was the deep wallet pocket where he kept his passport, traveller's cheques, airline tickets, etc. The right-hand pocket was smaller and too high up for comfort. A passport in that pocket would dig into his armpit.

'But if you changed while it was hanging up . . . ?' Annie suggested.

Salter sat on the bed and reconstructed the sequence of events when he undressed the night before. 'No,' he said. 'I put it in the left-hand pocket and then took it off. Someone's been in here.'

'Have we lost anything?'

They went over their possessions quickly. Nothing was missing. Even a wad of Canadian money was still there in the top of the suitcase.

'You must be wrong,' Annie said.

'No, I'm not,' Salter said. 'But if you don't believe me, no one else will. Okay. Put all this stuff together and I'll give it to the hotel to look after.'

Downstairs he found the landlord in his office and handed over his valuables to be put in the safe. On the spur of the moment he asked, 'Does anyone have access to the room when we're out?'

'How do you mean, sir?' Then: 'Something missing?'

'No, no. I just wondered.'

'Your room is perfectly safe, Mr Salter. The cleaning lady, Mrs Peabody, is totally reliable. Do you have any reason to think someone has been in? Apart from Mrs Peabody?'

'My passport was in the wrong place. But we are pretty careless. I probably forgot where I put it. I wouldn't want to lose anything, though.'

'You won't. One of us is around all the time. Here's a receipt for the valuables. Dinner tonight?'

'Yes, please. And every night we are here.'

'How long would that be?'

'A few days, I think. My wife likes it here.'

'Good.' He nodded to dismiss Salter.

All right, Salter thought. But you took that a bit calmly. No noisy defence of the hotel's honesty. Now we have a prowler, a peeper (or rather, a listener), and someone going through the room. All standard items in English country life?

Dinner was again superb. During it, Henry jumped at the chance of a day at the races, and Maud and Annie planned their next day's outing. The Canadian woman took her usual place, but Maud was more interested in the progress of Mario, the waiter, with the American girl. They were getting along well.

'Have you ever been picked up by a waiter?' Maud asked Annie.

'No. I was a waitress once and I got picked up by a customer. Him,' she said pointing at Salter. This was a slightly inaccurate version of how Salter had found her when she was helping to manage a resort hotel in Prince Edward Island, owned along with a lot of other enterprises, by her family, one of the leading families on the Island.

'Really,' Maud said. 'How romantic. Henry found me in a library. He came in every day for three months and then put in a request for me on a call slip. Look, I think he's propositioning her.'

They all looked around covertly. The American girl was nodding to the waiter and looking at her watch as she stood up. The waiter moved to another table, looking pleased.

'I wonder what language they use,' Annie

said. 'He doesn't speak much English.'

'Italian,' Maud said promptly. 'She's a graduate student, studying romance languages. I got chatting to her before dinner in the bar.'

'You interrogated her,' Henry said. 'She's twenty-two, unmarried, studying at Cornell, and her home is in Ithaca. New York, that is.'

Later, in bed, Annie said, 'How long do you think before Maud finds out you are a copper? This is getting a bit of a strain.'

'No, it isn't. It's fun. I told her this morning what a wonderful safety record we have. The bus company, I mean. She's nearly convinced, or defeated, which is the same thing. I thought I'd send her a card from the office when we get home. An official one. Her first failure. Now let's give that Listening Tom his money's worth.'

Two new arrivals appeared at breakfast the following day, a man and a woman in their thirties dressed as twins in identical blue jeans and windbreakers.

'They're not English,' Maud said. 'They look too much at home, and they aren't taking any notice of the rest of us. Perhaps more of your compatriots, Charlie.'

Breakfast was served by the Smarmy Boy, and Maud put the question to him.

'Australians, I think, madam. I'll find out for sure.'

Miss Rundstedt arrived, and Maud pointed out to Annie that she was either divorced or widowed.

'How can you tell?' Salter asked.

'It's a matter of rings, Charlie,' Annie said, slightly embarrassed. Mario put his head around the door and exchanged signals with the American girl, who got up quickly and left the room.

'Well, that's that,' Maud said. 'We might as well go now. We'll take our car and Henry and Charlie can go in yours.'

Salter went into the lounge to read the racing page of *The Times* while he waited for Henry, and watched, through the window, the American girl and Mario leave in her car. After ten minutes, when Henry still had not appeared, Salter went up to his room to organize his own needs for the day. He considered putting a hair across the door of the wardrobe, but when he tried he was unable to get it to stay in place. He tried spit and scotch tape until the area around the invisible hair began to look slightly wrecked, and he abandoned the idea, wiped the door clean and joined Henry.

The two men had a lot of time to kill so Salter fabricated an excuse and dropped Henry off at a bookshop while he 'did some errands'. He strolled casually into the police station, made a feeble inquiry about directions, and left. The sergeant joined him on the steps.

'You did it, did you, sir?' he asked, looking thoughtfully down the street.

'Yes. Got one for today?'

The sergeant's eyebrows went up. 'You are a sportsman, sir. But if you insist, yes. Try Licensed Guide. Should be good odds. First time out this year. My nephew's a stable lad there.'

'Right. By the way, Sergeant, when you were looking into the background of my host, did you find out where he learned Italian? And anything about what he was doing before he came here? What did he do for a living?'

'No, to both, sir. Why? Something fishy about him?'

'Just curious. Nothing to bother your

inspector about but he seems to keep well out of the way.'

'I understand, sir. I'll have another peek at the file. Best of luck now, sir. Think you can remember it?'

'Licensed Guide. I'll write it down. Keep your fingers crossed.'

After a short stroll around the town, Salter bought all the other morning papers and settled down to ham rolls in the Eagle and Child, where he had arranged to meet Henry. He read the papers carefully, underlining his selections as he had seen others do. He looked for horses with omens in their names, like Annie's Choice, and he found plenty; his real difficulty was that he could find significant omens in about half the horses in each race. He sat at the short end of the L-shaped bar, and when he looked up he was surprised to see the Canadian woman at the far end of the room. He considered speaking, decided against it, and leaned into the corner of the bar where he was shielded from view by a row of mugs hanging down from a rail above the bar. He was watching her composedly drinking when the door opened behind her and his racing acquaintance of the day before entered.

Parrott looked around the bar and Salter very nearly came out of hiding when the man caught the woman's eye and walked over to her table. She smiled at him and he sat down.

'Make a lovely couple don't they, sir,' a voice in his ear said. It was the barman, polishing glasses and looking at Salter in ironic complicity. 'Very sociable type, she is,' the barman said.

'I know her,' Salter said to cut him off. 'She's staying at the same place I am.'

'Boomewood, sir? I wouldn't be surprised if she moves a little closer to the centre, soon.' He looked pointedly across the room, and Salter, following his gaze, watched Parrott pat her knee.

'They come in here a lot, sir.'

'Do they?' Salter said. He guessed, like the barman, that she got patted a lot, but his reaction was to feel a small dislike for the barman for not keeping his observations to himself. And after all, the woman was a Canadian.

He shook out his paper and tried once more to make sense of English racing jargon. Henry appeared and ate his lunch and it was time for them to go.

Henry drove, and Salter carefully guided him over the route that Parrott had taken him the day before, right down to the rail by the first fence. He explained about watching the horses jump one fence, and how they would see the rest of the races from the stands.

'You've really got your feet under the table,' Henry said. 'Now show me about bookies. You know, I've never been to the races before.'

They crossed the course into the stands and Salter showed Henry how to bet, and where. Licensed Guide was in the second race and had no trouble romping home at odds of six to one. After the fourth race, they were joined for a while by Parrott. Salter had noticed his car parked near their own, and noticed, also, the Canadian woman who stayed in the car throughout the afternoon, but some small delicacy concerning what Maud would certainly make of it had held him back from pointing her out to Henry.

Now Parrott appeared at his elbow. 'Getting the hang of it?' he asked.

'Hullo,' said Salter, and introduced Henry. The three men chatted until it was time to bet and Salter moved off to find a bookmaker. The race began while he was still putting on his bet and he walked down to the rail to watch the horses sweep by for the first circuit. When he got back to Henry, Parrott was just leaving. No one had picked the winner.

Salter found two more winners, and the only flaw in the afternoon was that Henry, at the first race-meeting of his life, picked a winner in the third race with his first try and became an instant expert, explaining to Salter how to pick them out. Happily, when he had no more luck he shut up, and Salter could enjoy himself.

On the way home Henry said, 'What does your friend do for a living?'

'He's a building inspector, or some such. Why?'

'I just wondered. He certainly wanted to know all about you.'

'He's lonely, Henry. He's lived in Canada. I'm the first white man he's met around here. Old home week.'

'Yes? He sounded to me as if he was pumping me.'

'What did you tell him?'

'I told him you were probably a CIA

agent, posing as a bus conductor.'

'For the last time, Henry, I'm a Canadian. The CIA is American. Anyway, he doesn't look mysterious to me. Just lonely.'

'Really? You forget I'm married to an expert interrogator, Charlie.'

'Yes, and it's made you pretty good at it, Henry. And now I'll tell you what you talked about, shall I? *You* asked him if I seemed like a maintenance supervisor, didn't you? So what did he tell you?'

Henry blushed. 'I just like to do Maud in the eye sometimes, Charlie. As a matter of fact he said you seemed to be just the type.' Henry paused. 'But I tell you he *was* pumping me.'

Salter considered this. He was certain that he had never met Parrott before, but a lonely man on holiday will scrape an acquaintance wherever he can, and the policeman guessed that if he had lunch at the Eagle and Child the next day the man would be there, eager to be invited to the races again.

77

Two
Death in Tokesbury Mallett

At breakfast next morning the dining-room exploded. The Salters were late down and Maud and Henry had given their orders to the Smarmy Boy. He brought the Beresfords their eggs and took orders from the Salters. 'I'll do my best, sir and ma'am,' he said. 'But there's trouble in the kitchen – would you like some marmalade, Mrs Beresford? – so I can't promise anything.' He smiled at the Salters, then at the Beresfords, and left.

'Trouble in the kitchen?' Maude asked.
'Our hostess *is* the kitchen. We are lost without her. Hullo, here's the answer.'

Mario, the handsome waiter, had appeared in the doorway in street clothes with a suitcase in his hand, looking around the room. He spotted the American girl and walked over to her table and began a long conversation in a whisper. The girl rose to

78

her feet in evident distress and responded in Italian.

'This is maddening,' Maud observed.

Soon the waiter was shaking his head and the girl burst into tears. Dillon appeared in the doorway and said something sharply to Mario, who responded angrily. Then the American girl seemed to be arguing with Dillon. Mrs Dillon appeared from the kitchen and joined the girl in pleading with her husband while Mario stayed silent. Suddenly Mario turned on the host and shouted at him for about a minute, pointing to the Canadian woman, at which Mrs Dillon turned on her husband and began cursing him. The American girl ran out of the room in tears, followed by Mario, leaving the landlord and his wife arguing and pointing to Miss Rundstedt, who was now staring at them. Next the host grabbed his wife and pushed her out of the room, still shouting. There was a silence like the end of an artillery duel.

'I think we should leave,' Annie said.

'Are you out of your mind?' Maud cried, lenses flashing. 'Gregory,' she called. 'Come here. What's going on? Everything, please.'

Gregory was full of it. 'As far as I can tell,

ma'am, Mr Dillon has just given Mario the sack because he says he won't have his hotel made into a— excuse me, ma'am— knocking shop. The American lady says it was her fault and quite innocent— I'm sure it was— so it's not fair that Mario should have to lose his job. Poor old Mario. He's only got a work permit for this place, you see. He'll have to go back to Italy now. But the boss is insisting. He suspects Mario of ending up in one or two other beds in the past.'

The Prowler, thought Salter.

'What about the other bit? What was all that between our landlord and his wife?' Maud demanded.

Before Gregory could answer, the landlady appeared and slapped a piece of paper on the table in front of Miss Rundstedt and folded her arms aggressively across her bosom. 'You want to know why this is?' she screamed. But Miss Rundstedt grabbed the paper and rushed past the hostess out of the room.

Gregory returned. 'Carry on,' Maud said.

'Poor old Mario, he didn't like being fired,' Gregory said. 'So he accused the boss of being a hypocrite. Said he's been having it off with Miss Rundstedt. He's seen the boss coming out of her room more than once. He didn't say anything before because he didn't want to upset his sister, but I suppose it just slipped out now. A pity, really. These things are best left unsaid, don't you think so, ma'am?'

But he was talking to the wrong person. 'More,' Maud demanded.

'Well, the boss's wife has just told Miss Rundstedt to pack her bags, and the boss is having a terrible argument with his wife now in the kitchen. I'm afraid your eggs are spoilt, sir. Shall I get you some more bread?'

Salter nodded. Maud stopped the boy as he was leaving. 'What will this do to our dinner?' she wanted to know.

'I'll find out, ma'am,' he said. He returned almost immediately. 'No dinner tonight, I'm afraid,' he said. 'Now Mrs Dillon is packing her bags. Such a shame, really.'

The two Australians came over to their table. 'Fill us in, would you, mate?' the man said. 'What's up?'

Salter deferred to Maud, who supplied an already-polished account of the last twenty minutes.

'Christ!' the Australian said. 'And we were just thanking our stars for finding this place. I suppose we might as well shove off, too.'

Annie had been considering this. 'I wouldn't,' she said. 'This place without dinner is still better than most places with it.' She looked at Maud interrogatively, who nodded. 'We'll stay and see what happens.'

Suits me, thought Salter. One more day over the sticks.

'Right, Jilly?' the Australian asked his wife, who smiled her agreement. 'See you later, then,' he said to the table.

'Hang on a moment,' Maud said. 'Have you met our landlord? Is he Australian? We can't place his accent.' Thus incorporating the whole table in her nosiness.

'We thought he was a Yank,' the man said.

'That's it,' Annie said. 'He sounds like one of those English actors on television trying to do an American accent.'

'Well, well, well,' Maud said. 'No dinner, but what a lovely breakfast. Would you have thought it of our host? One never saw him above stairs until this morning but he hardly looks the type. I'm surprised at Miss Rundstedt, too. We saw her in town with another man and they certainly looked like an item. What a lot of pigs you men are,' she added irrelevantly. 'Ah, well. I've never understood adultery. No one ever gives me the chance.

Come on, Henry. See you outside, Annie.'

Salter had been granted his wish for one more day at the races, and Henry had chosen to accompany the women again, so he went off to read the papers while everyone else got ready to leave. From the lounge he heard the argument in the kitchen continuing, but quieter now, and at ten o'clock Mrs Dillon appeared without her coat and Salter assumed she had been persuaded to stay. He watched the departure of all the other guests and witnessed one last kiss between Mario and the American girl before she drove off with her luggage.

He decided that the local police ought to know about this morning's events because they were probably, in one way or another, connected with the prowler or the listener. He also wanted to have a word with the sergeant.

'Hullo, again, Charles,' Churcher greeted him. 'I was mentioning you to my wife last night, and we were wondering if you and your wife would care to have a bit of dinner with us while you're here.'

'That would be nice,' Salter said. 'I'll ask my wife what our plans are. I dropped by to tell you that I think you can close your file on the Boomewood Prowler.' He told Churcher the story of the morning's excitement; the inspector wrote it all down on a pad of foolscap paper.

'Hmm,' he said, ticking off the sentences as he re-read them. 'You think, then, that our Italian lad got into the wrong bedroom?'

'I did at first. But it's possible that the landlord may be the one.'

'I see. You think this Canadian woman may be one among many, do you? Our landlord exercising a sort of *droit de seigneur* over his unattached female guests?'

'She may be the only one; she was staying there last week.'

'Right, I see,' Churcher said again. He considered for a few moments. 'Which, do you think?'

'I would say the landlord, on the evidence of the phrase "wakey-wakey". That's not an Italian expression.'

'True. But you know sometimes these fellows pick up the slang first. There was an Italian waiter at a little place we used to go to when I was courting my wife who began half his sentences with "Cor bloody blimey". We would order something and he would say, "Cor bloody blimey, signor, the veal isa the besta thing tonight." '

Salter laughed. 'Either way, it's probably an inside job. Now I've got to go. I'll ask my wife about dinner, but don't be offended if we leave tomorrow. She's very changeable.'

'Not at all. A woman's privilege. Keep in touch, though.'

Salter nodded to the sergeant on the way out and waited to be joined on the steps.

'What's the word for today, Sergeant?' he asked without preamble.

'Monkey's Paw looks good in the first, sir. What did you get about Licensed Guide?'

'Sixes,' Salter said.

'Ah,' the sergeant sighed. 'That's the advantage of being there, isn't it? It went off at fours. Cheers.' He disappeared inside the station, and Salter headed for the pub.

The bar was empty, and Salter ordered his beer and looked for Monkey's Paw among the runners.

'I hear there was a bit of bother at your place this morning, sir,' the barman said. 'The lady left in a bit of a rush, like.'

Salter felt a growing dislike for his confidant, and decided to risk the lunch at another pub in future. 'I heard the landlord made a pass at her,' he said. 'Not her fault, was it?'

'I see, sir. Defending her honour, was she?'

Salter sighed. By now the whole town was probably in on the gossip, but he felt sorry for the woman and a need to dissociate himself from the nudging matiness of the tapster. He said nothing, but picked up his paper to try to read what Our Newmarket Correspondent had to say. The barman took the hint and moved away, and when a small flurry of people came in, Salter left the remains of his beer and headed for the parking lot.

Monkey's Paw won and in four other races Salter picked the horse that came second, so that while he lost money he was pleased with his performance.

When the four of them assembled at Boomewood they learned that although Mrs Dillon was still in residence, she was taking the evening off and the dining-room was closed. They dined at the Swan, chewing the edges of some braised ox liver and turnips followed by cubes of a cake-like substance called cabinet pudding. Even Maud was too dispirited to make more than one bright remark about the alternative dessert, which was called 'Spotted Dick'. 'Ah,' she said. 'Dead Man's Leg in a Bandage.'

The waiter, a huge, toothless fellow of the type used to open the front door in gothic films, was surly because they had not taken his suggestions about the menu. 'I told you to 'ave the 'ot-pot,' he growled, as he cleared away the nearly untouched liver. 'You wouldn't listen!'

Afterwards they had drinks in the 'American Bar' where the barman tried to sell them his special.

'I think,' Annie said, without consulting Salter, 'that we might as well push on tomorrow.'

'Oh, give it a day,' Maud cried. 'Wait and see if Maria goes back to her kitchen. And if she is still sulking, there must be a Tweedledum to eat at somewhere.'

Annie looked at Salter. He was hers to dispose of, and he could see she was tempted. As she became familiar with the area, she became more and more interested in it and wanted to dig deeper. If they left now they would simply drive through the rain to another hotel, and so on the next day. Salter wondered if the police sergeant would know of somewhere in the same class as Boomewood. 'I'll ask around tomorrow,' he said. 'There must be somewhere.'

'You know people here?' the ever-alert Maud asked.

'I know a barman at a pub,' Salter parried. 'I'll ask him.'

So they decided to give Boomewood one more night and make a decision the next day.

In the event, the decision to leave Boomewood was made for them. In the early hours of the morning, Salter was awakened by a banging on the door from a dream in which he was eating a boiled sheepshead. He put on his raincoat and opened the door to the sergeant from Tokesbury Mallett. Outside there was the noise of cars arriving, doors opening, and voices in the hall.

'The Prowler?' Salter asked.

'A bit more serious than that, sir. Your landlord. He's dead. His wife stabbed him. Would you mind coming downstairs, sir, and making a statement?'

'Good Christ!' Salter said. 'You want my wife, too?'

'Yes, please, sir. In the residents' lounge,

please.' He moved along the hall to wake up the other guests.

They put on some clothes and descended to the lounge where the Beresfords and the Australians were already waiting. The only other person present was Gregory, who was offering to make everyone a cup of tea. Inspector Churcher had taken charge. As Salter arrived, he greeted him loudly. 'Charles,' he said. 'A bit of a busman's holiday for you, but I don't think I'll need any help. I'll brief you later, but right now I'd like to get a statement from everybody as to where you all were last night, what time you went to bed, whether you heard anything unusual, that sort of thing. I'd like you to do it one by one, please. The constable is waiting in the dining-room, so if you'd go in first, sir.' He nodded to the Australian.

Salter was very conscious of Maud's glasses trained on him and he turned to look at her.

'I'd have found out eventually,' she said. 'I never believed that bus company rubbish.'

Salter acknowledged the remark with a small inclination of the head, and Annie grinned. But now that someone had been killed, Salter felt less interested in larking about with Maud Beresford. He felt as if he had been acting in a brightly coloured travelogue, moving through the gentle, if rain-soaked, English countryside without really believing in it or taking the inhabitants seriously. A murder changed that: the film was black and white again, familiar and real.

Annie, watching him watching the proceedings, said, 'It's nothing to do with you, Charlie.'

'I know that,' Salter said. 'I'm just interested to see how they do it.'

He was the last to make a statement, and then Churcher sent everyone else back to bed with instructions to let him know before they left the district.

'I'll follow you up,' Salter said to Annie.

'Soon,' she said warningly.

The photographer left, along with the doctor and the ambulance men. Salter settled down at Churcher's invitation to another cup of tea with the inspector and the sergeant.

'Here's the story,' Churcher said. 'Quite clear-cut. Mrs Dillon was picked up about an hour ago driving erratically on the Oxford Road. The patrol car suspected she was drunk, but when he got a good look at her he saw blood on her clothes and her hands. She seemed hysterical, so they took her into custody and brought her back to us. Take over, Sergeant.'

'The constable on duty called me,' the sergeant said, 'and I had a little chat with her, calmed her down a bit, and then she told me she'd killed her husband. Just like that. So I called the inspector – I didn't really believe her – and we came up and found him.'

'Where? How?'

'The old pro, eh, Charles?' Churcher said. 'He was in his office along the hall. He was dead all right. The surgeon said he'd been stabbed seven or eight times. There was a lot of blood about.'

'What with? Does she carry a knife?'

'No. She used one that Dillon kept in a drawer, it seems. A memento of the war.'

'Where is it?'

'We haven't got it. She said she threw it away. She doesn't remember where, she says. We'll have a bit of a search, of course, but it might be anywhere. She was ten miles away when they stopped her. Of course, the weapon isn't really necessary, with her confession. A fairly simple matter, really.'

'Have you got a proper statement from her?'

'Not yet. We'll get that now, eh, Sergeant?'

'It's the next thing, sir, according to procedure.'

'Right. Well, Charles, a little story for you to take back to Toronto. But I imagine you get a lot of this with such a high percentage of foreigners.'

'Yes, it's the interesting English-type murders we miss. The ones where some railway clerk has fourteen middle-aged women buried in the basement.'

Churcher chuckled. 'Yes. Well, I must be off,' he said.

'Can I come by in the morning?' Salter asked. 'I'd like to hear her version of why she did it.'

'Oh, I think we all know the motive, Charles. Sexual jealousy, of course. All the people here witnessed that little scene the other morning. Yesterday, wasn't it?'

Salter nodded. 'You'll have to confirm that with the Rundstedt woman. We all got the same version from the Smarmy Boy and he was translating from the Italian.'

'From who?'

'Sorry. Gregory. The lad who made our tea.'

'Do we have Miss Rundstedt's address, Sergeant?'

'She's staying at one of the hotels in town, sir. She should be easy to find.'

'Right. Let's go, then, Sergeant. Busy day ahead.'

Churcher walked down the hall to the front door; Salter held the sergeant for a moment.

'This place will be closed after tonight,' he said. 'Where can we stay? Most of all, where can we get a decent meal?'

'Plain or fancy?' the sergeant asked.

'Plain.' 'Fancy', they had already learned, meant imitation French.

'The Plough,' Sergeant Robey said promptly. 'In Wartlock. About two miles down the road towards Marstonbury Edge. Roast beef, apple tart, their own eggs. And they have Hunter's bitter, sir.'

Churcher reappeared in the doorway looking for his sergeant.

'Thanks, Sergeant,' Salter said. To the inspector, he said, 'We'll need a place to stay. I was just asking the sergeant if he knew of anywhere. Can you recommend a place, Charles?'

Churcher posed thoughtfully, then shook his head. 'No, I suppose Sergeant Robey is your best man on that. Cheers, then.'

Poor bugger, thought Salter again. Nobody asks him anything.

In the morning they found a constable in charge of the hotel. Gregory made everyone tea, and the Australians left. Salter told the Beresfords about the Plough and they all agreed to try it for a night. The bill was easy to calculate and Gregory solemnly gave them all receipts, apologizing for the inconvenience of the murder. Annie and Maud had become addicted to a little book of 'walks' in the district and had decided on a long one that would take them most of the day. Henry wanted to 'nip back to Watford and look at my rats for an hour', and Salter, declining an offer to accompany the women, assured everyone that he would be quite happy mooching about the town.

The exterior of the Plough looked promising. It was built of grey stone, and the name was spelled out along the front of the hotel in fresh gold paint, a combination of colours that reminded Salter of the clock tower of Hart House in Toronto. The hotel faced the village green, and Salter guessed that the management took some responsibility for maintaining the green, a piece of pure Merrie England with a pond, ducks, and what looked like a monument to those who fell at Agincourt. The green sward blended perfectly with the grey and gold of the hotel, so perfectly that Salter decided that if he ever owned a racehorse, these would be his racing colours.

He led the way through the door, stumbled and tripped down two stone steps, and recovered to smash his head against a giant beam that served as a lintel over the inner door. The other three waited while he staggered about, then joined him in the lobby.

'Heeazeard abeuve, heeazeard beleough,' a voice said from inside the lobby.

'What was that?' Salter asked, his head ringing.

The owner of the voice stepped forward. A dapper little man in a blazer and brilliantly polished shoes. 'Heeazeard abeuve, heeazeard beleough,' he said again, pointing first at the lintel, then at the step. He executed a manœuvre with his feet that turned him sideways to them and pointed across the lobby at the desk.

'Ah,' Salter said and looked inquiringly at Maud. 'Sandhurst Oxbridge,' she whispered in his ear. 'The accent peculiar to army officers who have to shout.'

The landlady, behind the desk, smiled a welcome. A pleasant-looking, fat little lady, she signed them in, organized their luggage and showed them to their rooms, all the while her husband stood guard by the door.

As they learned later, she cooked the meals, kept the place shining, and generally made life agreeable for the guests, while her husband looked after the outside of the hotel and the bar. His accent, however, intensified as the day went on and in the late evening Salter and Annie needed Maud to translate for them. He had one other habit that was especially disconcerting when he was away from the bar. He preferred to conduct all conversations with a rigid back at a two-hundred and seventy degree angle from his guests; occasionally he veered around until he was virtually back to back, and talking to him was like playing a stylized scene in a comedy of the Thirties. Otherwise, it turned out, there was everything to recommend the place.

By ten o'clock that morning, Salter was once more chatting to Churcher in his office.

'She had gone to see *Romeo and Juliet,*' Churcher said. 'When she got back, quite late, I gather, though she doesn't know the time, she and Dillon got into an argument again, over the Rundstedt woman, and one thing led to another and she stabbed him. A bit operatic, but these people are not like us, are they?'

'And then she decided to run away? Why the Oxford road?'

'It joins in with the London road. She said she was going back home to Italy.'

Salter said, 'There were six of us and the Smarmy Boy around. Maybe we were all asleep but nobody heard anything. There couldn't have been much of a row.'

Churcher shrugged. 'I think that just goes to show. When you know who the culprit is, and they confess, you don't have to worry about all the odd little bits, do you? She has signed a statement, after proper warning, of course.'

'Have you talked to Rundstedt yet?'

'Of course. She confirmed the row. Says that Dillon did visit her in her room a couple of times. She didn't see any harm in it, she says. Not on holiday.'

'I see. Where is she now?'

'Staying at the Swan. Why?'

'On her own?'

Churcher looked at Salter in surprise, and with a touch of embarrassment. 'She is now,' he said. 'But when we spoke to her there was someone else with her.'

'A man named Jeremy Parrott?'

'Yes. Apparently a one-night stand. He left this morning. You seem very interested in her, Charles. Fancy her yourself?' Churcher arranged a knowing leer on his face.

It was a silly remark, and Salter forgave him for it. It must be irritating to have some smart-aleck 'colonial' copper anticipate you. 'Not really,' Salter said. 'She gets around too much.' He had a thought. 'I suppose there's no chance I could talk to Mrs Dillon, or watch you talk to her.'

' "No" to both. I remember you asked about that last night, but it's against the proper form and besides she isn't here. We've transferred her to the regional headquarters where they have proper facilities for women prisoners.'

'So that's that, then.'

'Yes,' Churcher said. 'My first murder in this posting. My first real murder, as a matter of fact. Nice to have it all tickety-boo. No credit to me, of course, but it looks well. At the end of the day, that's what counts, isn't it.'

I hope so, for your sake, Salter thought. It was, of course, like nine out of ten homicides in its typical motive, its 'in-house' suspect, and the lack of any real mystery, but Salter was troubled by it. What bothered him was the apparent lack of any detail or witness that would confirm Mrs Dillon's account. And there was a very big disparity between the angry woman they had seen the day before, the woman who had kicked out Miss Rundstedt, and a killer who inflicts seven or eight stab wounds. But she had confessed, and if Churcher had done a solid job on her statement, there was no point in going behind it. Churcher had a right to feel pleased.

'May they all be like this,' Salter said, and stood up.

There being no racing he was in no hurry

for lunch, but the pubs were open and habit took him into the Eagle and Child. He regretted his choice as soon as he saw the barman, who welcomed him as a regular.

'Lots of excitement at your place last night, sir,' the barman said.

'Oh? What do you hear?' Salter asked.

'I hear your landlady did in her old man, sir.'

'That's what you heard, is it?' Salter asked politely.

'That's what they tell me. Trouble over a lady, I hear,' he said.

'You hear a lot,' Salter said, and stared at the barman. He got his effect as the barman went back to polishing his glasses and moved away. Salter went back to his beer in silence. He left the bar and walked over to the Swan for lunch, where the 'ploughman's lunch' consisted of a bun and a piece of cracked orange cheese accompanied by a stick of celery. While he nibbled on these, he inquired casually of the barman if he knew if Miss Rundstedt was still at the hotel, saying he wanted to look her up. He saw the barman go wary and knew that the whole town knew the story. 'She's still here, sir,' the barman said. 'In there, having lunch.'

He pointed through the glass doors to the dining-room where Miss Rundstedt could be seen at a table not twenty feet away.

'I won't bother her now,' Salter said. 'I'll surprise her later.'

The barman nodded and moved away. When Salter left the bar, he felt the man's eyes on his back, and knew that the barman would have an extra detail to tell anyone who cared to listen. On the other hand, he thought it was unlikely that anyone in this town would keep Churcher in touch with the local gossip, so that the knowledge that 'some American' was snooping around would probably die before it reached the inspector's office.

Salter drove back to the Plough where he tried to make up for his disturbed night with a little nap. He woke up at four and went down to the residents' lounge in search of a cup of tea or coffee, and had an agreeably absurd conversation back to back with his host. When Henry and the women returned they all had a pint of Hunter's bitter and an early dinner of steak pie and apple tart and cream which made them happy to have found a home again.

'Been sleuthing, Charlie?' Maud asked,

over some more beer.

'You think they'd let me poke my nose in?' Salter asked.

'I just wondered,' Maud said. 'Of course, you may not be a policeman at all. That may be one of your many disguises. I must say Annie is extremely well got up for a policeman's wife.'

'Oh, Maud. I told you. I have my own job.'

Salter turned the conversation around. 'I'll show you my passport in the morning,' he said. 'And my official identification, if you like.'

'She'll say it's just a clever piece of cover,' Henry said.

'It's so hard with you colonials,' Maud said. 'You can't tell a thing from the accent – at least, I can't.' Salter thought about something Maud had said to him two days before. 'What sort of accent did our host at Boomewood have, under the American act?' he asked. 'Upper, middle, lower, or one of the eleven in between. See, I'm learning.'

Maud laughed. 'Aren't you, though. My guess would be that he was a grammar school boy. He wore all the old school tie

102

gear, but it was all a bit wobbly, like his accent. There was something else about the way he spoke too. He used a lot of out-of-date phrases, like a Rip Van Winkle. Or like one of those German spies during the war who mugged up their English from old Bull-dog Drummond stories.'

'Did he seem like a lecher to you?'

'Nobody makes passes at me, Charlie, I told you. Though if they came at me when I didn't have my glasses on I'd be helpless. But that's an odd thing. I can usually tell who would and who wouldn't – we all can, can't we, Annie? – and I was quite surprised when the row blew up over the Rundstedt woman. Weren't you, Annie?'

'I never saw the man except during the row,' Annie said. 'Now, knock it off, Charlie. I want to talk about tomorrow. If we stay here I want to do some shopping for the boys, and I want you to come with me.'

'All right. Where do you want to go?'

'Cheltenham,' Annie said. 'It's a long drive but we missed it on the way through and I hear they have good shops there.'

'What's the forecast?' Salter asked. 'Sunny with cloudy periods, or cloudy with sunny periods?'

'It's going to piss down,' Henry said. 'You might as well go shopping.'

'Are we going to spend the rest of our time here with Maud and Henry?' Salter asked as they tramped around Cheltenham in a steady drizzle. 'We seem to have become a foursome.'

'They like us, Charlie, and I like them,' Annie said. 'We can take off anytime we want, but there's no need to be wary of them.'

'It's a bit un-English, isn't it?' Salter grumbled. 'I thought they were supposed to be stand-offish.'

'Haven't you noticed, Charlie? The English are either very stand-offish or friendly as hell. There are two kinds, you see—'

'Oh, don't start that, again. Come on. Let's buy Angus that Swiss army knife and get out of here. The main street in that village we went through is about ten feet wide and I want to be through there before the rush-hour starts when the shepherds quit.'

'But you can get Swiss army knives in Toronto!'

'I know. Probably cheaper, too. But he

hasn't got one, has he?'

Down came the rain. At dinner that night even Maud was slightly depressed. The forecast was glum but there was still no point in driving north to sit in another hotel. On the other hand, while Maud and Annie had uncovered a huge layer of interesting activities in the neighbourhood — market days, horse fairs, and such — nothing was very much fun in the rain.

'Let's go up to town,' Maud suggested.

'Where's that?' Salter asked.

'London, idiot.'

The prospect of having a look at London while the women shopped would normally have pleased Salter, but he had developed new priorities. In Cheltenham, he had picked up a racing diary and discovered that while racing was over at Tokesbury Mallett, it was just beginning at Burford. By comparing the diary with a map, he had uncovered the wonderful information that the authorities had so arranged things that there was a race meeting somewhere every day within a reasonable drive. And he had come to enjoy standing up to his ankles in mud, with the rain trickling down his neck, trying to find the bookie with the best odds.

'You go,' he said. 'I might watch *Pot the Black*. One of our boys looks like winning it.'

Annie looked at him thoughtfully. Salter had never played pool in his life to her knowledge, and spending the afternoon watching anything on television was completely out of character. Salter returned her gaze blandly.

'All right,' she said at last. So it was agreed.

'What are you up to?' she asked, when they were in bed.

'Who, me? Nothing?'

'Don't get addicted,' she said. 'As long as it's raining, I'm glad the racing is keeping you cheerful, but when the sun comes out, I want us to start having a holiday together.'

But Salter did not go to the races. When he called in at the police station the next morning for a tip from the sergeant, and to thank him for recommending the Plough, he found Churcher looking glum.

'Area headquarters are getting involved,' he told Salter. 'Apparently they don't like the woman's statement. They've raised a number of questions.'

106

'What's wrong with it? Did they say?'

'Inconsistencies, they said.' He looked at Salter worriedly. 'They think the confession may be false. As a matter of fact they've released her.'

Salter said nothing. He felt sorry for Churcher.

'I'm expecting someone this afternoon, a Superintendent Hamilton. Would you mind coming in to meet him? He'll be here at three o'clock. You may be able to tell him something I've missed. I seem to have missed a lot.' Churcher looked at his hands.

'Sure,' Salter said. 'He'll probably tell me to get my ass out of here, though. I would if I were him.'

'Did you have any inkling that the Dillon woman might be lying? I mean, why the hell should she?'

'I never spoke to her, did I?' Salter said. Should he tell Churcher that he had smelt something wrong from the start? No. 'What next?' he asked, standing up.

Churcher shrugged and avoided Salter's gaze. 'It's out of my hands now.'

'I'll see you this afternoon,' Salter said.

There was no point in talking to the sergeant now, and Salter headed directly for the

Eagle and Child, risking the barman's confidences for the sake of the food.

'All alone today, sir,' the barman said as he brought his beer.

'I always am,' Salter said, surprised.

'No, sir. I mean in here.' Salter looked around. The bar was empty.

'She left about an hour ago, sir,' the barman confided. 'I saw her drive off from the Swan as I was getting some change from the bank.'

To ask 'who' would have been pointless. Salter grunted and sipped his beer.

'I expect things are a bit quiet for her at the Swan,' the barman offered. 'She seems to like a lot of action.'

Suddenly Salter had had enough. 'Why don't you keep your goddam observations to yourself,' he suggested. 'Or save them for your memoirs.' For a moment the barman looked as if he was going to respond in kind, and Salter picked up his beer and waited. But the arrival of another customer gave the barman reason for breaking away, and he stayed at the far end of the bar, contenting himself with casting sour glances along the bar from time to time.

Superintendent Hamilton was seated at Churcher's desk when Salter walked in. Churcher was standing beside the desk with his hands clasped behind him.

He was perhaps sixty, with a ragged ginger-and-grey fringe of hair around a weatherbeaten bald head. His face was like a piece of rock, patchily coloured as if the sun had not penetrated all the crevices. His eyes were small and very close together, which should have made him look devious but because of their piercing quality created a shotgun effect. He fixed Salter in his sights. 'The Toronto copper, eh?' he said. 'Salter? My name is Hamilton, Wylie Hamilton. Take a chair and tell me what you think of all this. Bugger orf for a bit, would you, Churcher? You've heard all this before, and besides, you might intimidate Salter here.' He twisted his mouth to show he was joking, and stared at Churcher until the inspector left.

What class said 'orf' instead of 'off', Salter wondered. Hamilton looked and acted like a squire, but he must have been a constable at some point or could you start above the ranks in this mob, if you had the right background and said 'orf' instead of 'off'?

'Your man has handled this thing very well,' Salter offered. 'I was impressed by . . .'

Hamilton cut him off. 'I don't want to know what you think of Churcher,' he said. 'Tell me what you saw and heard. *Then* you can tell me what to think.'

Salter went over the events from his point of view, from the row over Miss Rundstedt to the death of Dillon. 'It looks pretty clear to me, as it did to Churcher,' he finished.

'It's a balls-up and you know it,' Hamilton snarled. 'If you had handled anything like this, Orliff would have kicked your arse through your hat.'

Orliff was Salter's superior in Toronto. Salter tried not to react immediately. 'You know him?' he asked, appearing to register the name only casually.

'I've had dealings with him,' Hamilton said.

'And you've been in touch with him?'

'I phoned him this morning. Got him out of bed. Apparently it was five o'clock in the morning, eskimo time.' Hamilton smiled briefly. Then he said, 'He told me you're not a complete bloody fool.'

'Did he also tell you that I am on holiday?'

'The people at the Plough told me you are staying for the next two days. I don't need your help, Salter, but it would be nice to have someone to talk to.' Hamilton's reference was clear. 'All right?' he asked.

'Sure.' Salter shrugged. 'So what's happened? Has Mrs Dillon retracted her statement?'

'Her what? Retracted her what? What bloody statement? Have you seen it?'

Salter shook his head. It was clear that whatever Hamilton's natural manner was, he was now very angry.

'The bloody statement broke down at the first sentence. You wouldn't need a lawyer from London. One of the local toss-pots could do it. Here.' He tossed the statement across the desk.

'Now,' he said. 'I don't know how they do it in Saskatchewan . . .'

'Ontario,' Salter said.

'Wherever. But in this country when a hysterical woman confesses to murdering her husband — immediately, mind you, not under questioning or anything, in pidgin English — we try to make sure she's telling the truth.'

'She was caught running away,' Salter

111

pointed out. 'Covered in blood.'

'From what, eh? From what? Churcher!' he shouted. 'Bring us some tea, will you?'

When the tea arrived, and Churcher had been dismissed, Hamilton resumed.

'We took her over her statement,' he said. 'And every time it came out differently. First she said they quarrelled right away. Then she said they had a long talk, maybe an hour, before they quarrelled. Then she said she stabbed him as he was sitting in the chair. Then she said she stabbed him in the back. And the knife!' Hamilton squinted at the statement. 'He kept a knife in his bedroom. First she says she ran upstairs and got it and came back down to kill him with it. So I asked her why she locked the bedroom door after her. We tripped her up on every single, sodding, sentence.'

'You think she's lying, then?'

'I know she's lying, laddie. I know she's lying. But why?'

'Did she go to the play?'

'Oh, she went to the play all right. We found a pal she went with. An Italian woman. And you know what? Her husband was killed when Romeo was getting his in the tomb.'

'How do you know?'

'We asked the surgeon, laddie. We asked the bloody surgeon to establish the time of death. Dillon was killed while you lot were roistering in the Swan. Churcher did not even bother to check the surgeon's report. They hardly exchanged two words! Christ Almighty!'

To divert him from his fury, Salter said, 'She's covering for someone, obviously.'

'Obviously. Obviously. Obviously. Who?'

'Her brother?'

'Ah. Got there, have we?'

Screw you, thought Salter. Up until now he had been intrigued by Hamilton, but he had no intention of trotting alongside the Englishman's stirrup, being catechized.

'Well?' Hamilton barked.

Salter shrugged. 'So find the brother,' he said.

'He's disappeared. We have an all points bulletin out— is that what you call it? Any other suggestions?'

'Italy.'

Hamilton shook his head. 'We've tried that. He hasn't gone home, or he's not there yet.'

'Ask his sister. She might know.'

'Of course she knows, but she won't tell us. She says she has no idea.'

'So keep asking her. Churcher tells me you've released her. You had some charges that would stick; she's your only lead to her brother. Why take the chance that she'll disappear, too?'

'You underestimate my enormous cunning, old son. I'm not taking any chances on that one. I have installed a bright young constable in the ditch outside her hotel with instructions to follow the lady wherever she goes. He's got a big picture of her brother in his pocket, too, so that he can check up on any visitors that may call. The idea is, you see, that if she thinks we are no longer interested in her, she might just lead us to the brother. Not fearfully subtle but a bit better than what you give me credit for. Any other suggestions?'

'The American girl.'

'Who?'

'The American girl. Her name is in the register. She and the brother were lovers, or something. Very close, anyway. He may have told her where he was going. I saw them kissing goodbye in the parking lot.'

'And right now she's somewhere in

England, or Scotland, or buggered orf altogether, I suppose.'

'You have her car licence number from the register at Boomewood – Dillon was fussy about that – she rented from the same company I'm using, so they could give you a complete description. All these little cars look alike to me.'

Hamilton mused. 'That's a bit of help. I'll put a trace on her. Put her on the fucking computer.'

Salter looked at his watch. 'Hold on. Can I borrow your phone for a minute?'

Hamilton pushed the instrument across the desk. Salter dialled Information and got the phone number of the Plough, then dialled again. He was answered immediately. 'Hyelleough?' the voice said.

'Mr Stiles? Charlie Salter here. Do you know if my wife is back from London yet?'

'All here present and correct, swilling tea,' Stiles shouted. 'You'd like a word with your CO?'

Salter worked out what Stiles had said. 'No,' he said. 'Let me speak to Maud Beresford if she's there.' He looked up at Hamilton who was ringing his ear furiously with his index finger. 'Ah, Maud. You remember the American girl? Mario's girlfriend? Yeah. Do you know where she headed for when she left that morning? Good. Hang on.'

Hamilton took his finger out and pushed a pad of paper across the desk at Salter.

'Okay,' Salter resumed. 'Cranmer House, Gosforth, Seascale, Cumberland. And the name? c/o Gush. Thanks.' He put the phone down. 'You'll find her here,' he said to Hamilton. 'Staying with some people called Gush.' Good old Maud.

'You keep track of everybody?' Hamilton asked, impressed.

'She gave her address to a woman who is staying at the Plough with us.'

'Huh.' Hamilton transcribed Salter's note into a form he could pass on. The door opened as he was writing and a man in his thirties in plain clothes entered.

'Ah, Woodiwiss,' Hamilton said. 'Inspector Salter of the Toronto police. Detective-Sergeant Woodiwiss.'

Woodiwiss glanced at Salter and nodded. 'We've completed the search,' he said. 'We found this.' He threw an envelope on to the table.

Hamilton opened the envelope and drew out a thick wad of twenty-pound notes. 'How

116

many would you say?' he asked.

'Fifty, sir.'

'Skimming, was he?'

The sergeant shrugged. It was not up to him to speculate and maybe get skewered for it by Hamilton.

'All right.' Hamilton nodded. 'I think that's it, Salter, until we get hold of Miss America. If you have any more thoughts, share them with me, will you? I'm at the Swan.'

Good, thought Salter maliciously. Enjoy the 'ot-pot. He left the office and was intercepted by a slightly forlorn-looking Churcher who was putting on a show of activity at the front desk.

'Fierce old devil, isn't he?' Churcher said. 'I hear he's like that with everybody. Can't take offence, eh?'

'He's a type,' Salter said comfortingly. 'Don't let him bother you.' After Salter's twenty minutes with Hamilton, Churcher seemed to have a slight cockney accent. At any rate he was now sure that 'orf' was upper.

'Thanks Maud,' Salter said at dinner. 'Your professional curiosity was very

117

helpful. Made me look good.'

Maud said, 'Don't be rude. It wasn't pure nosiness this time. The girl was very miserable and I was just trying to be helpful. Now what's on the agenda for tomorrow?'

'I'll just tag along with you two,' Annie said. 'Charlie's on a case.'

'Knock it off, Annie. I just happen to be a copper and these people feel more comfortable asking me whether it was raining on the night of whatever-it-was. That's all.'

Annie said nothing.

'How far is Coventry?' Henry asked, interrupting the silence. 'I'd like to see the cathedral.'

They consulted the landlord. More than an hour, less than two, Maud translated, because the road zigzagged across country. Maud and Henry decided to go, and Annie asked to be allowed to join them. Salter said nothing, his desire to stay in touch with Hamilton overcoming the need to be nice to Annie.

The next morning, when Salter was alone after breakfast, he was interrupted in his attempt to answer a single clue in *The Times* crossword puzzle by Hamilton on the telephone. 'We've found Miss America,' Hamilton said, 'and she's driving down immediately. She's heard the news and thinks we are jumping to conclusions, I gather.'

'We don't want to do that, do we?' Salter said, enjoying the opportunity to be flippant to a senior officer. 'What are we going to do now?'

'Sit here and scratch my bum. Come and talk to me, unless you plan to be funny.'

Salter arrived at the station in time for coffee, and Churcher brought him a cup, hanging about the office until Hamilton thanked him pointedly. I'll have to accept that dinner invitation, Salter thought.

'I've been looking at this hotel register,' Hamilton said. 'How long were you there?'

'Two days.'

'Hmm. What about that nosey-parker you phoned yesterday?'

'Maud Beresford? She'd been there over a week, I think.'

'Have her look at this register, will you? We will probably have to check them all the way back through March, but she might re-member something from her stay that would save us some trouble. Here. Show it to her, will you?' Hamilton threw the vital piece of evidence across the desk.

'What are we looking for?' Salter asked.

'She is trying to remember anything funny about the people who stayed there while she was around. Especially any rough-looking fellows who threatened our host.' Hamilton bared his teeth, and pulled another document to him. 'I'm not joking entirely. I've been looking over the history of our dead friend. It's interesting. We have no idea what he was doing from 1944 until 1978. Just his word as reported to us. According to the statement he gave to the War Office, in 1944 he was in a village in Tuscany, hiding out from the Germans. Apparently he had found himself behind the lines at some previous point and gone into hiding. When Jerry started to pull back and our people arrived, he came out of hiding and fiddled himself a psychological wound – loss of memory, shell shock – and got back to Blighty, where he disappeared. He was listed as "Missing, Presumed Dead", and certified as such in the records when no trace of him emerged. He gave himself a false identity and went underground, living on his wits, he said. An amnesty on deserters was declared after the war but he didn't come forward until 1978, when he was tried, given a conviction without penalty and formally discharged. Then he popped up here. He had obviously made a pisspotful of money because he bought Boomewood and spent a lot on it.'

'That accounts for the fact that he could speak Italian. Did he meet his wife there during the war?'

'No. She would have been a nipper, then. No. After he got his dry-cleaning job he took a sentimental journey back to—' here Hamilton consulted the document again— 'Valdottavo to see if he could find the people who had helped him during the war. That's when he met his wife. Swept her orf her feet, apparently. Brought her back to England and opened an Italian pensione. Was the food good?'

'Terrific.'

'Really? Do you know what I got at the Swan last night? Toad-in-the-hole.'

'What the hell is that?'

'Sausages in batter pudding. Yorkshire pudding to you. It can be good. This tasted like rancid lava-crust. But I'm getting off the point. This spring Mrs Dillon sent for her brother to help out. That's the story.'

'What was Dillon doing for thirty years?'

'The most likely thing is something crooked. He had no papers, though God knows, you can get some easily enough, so he probably worked the black economy. His wife knows nothing about it – he was in business, he told her – and the War Office didn't go behind his story; when the police tried to, he said he worked for day wages in the street markets. He probably did something of the sort, maybe in London. They say that on Sunday mornings along Petticoat Lane you can get your watch stolen at one end of the street and buy it back at the other, but I heard that story when I was in nursery school. It's true, though, that a lot of stolen goods find their way to the street markets and plenty of wide boys make a good living along the way.'

'It's possible, then, that he was still receiving, and hence the envelope you found.'

'Anything's possible, Salter, and I shall have to ask around to see if we can pick up a whisper. The thing is that Boomewood was doing well, he was respectable now, and something in his past may have caught up with him.'

'Blackmail?'

'Possible. Some villain with a grudge who got done when Dillon didn't. You see, the scope of this investigation is unlimited.' Hamilton spoke the word bitterly. 'A pity Churcher wasn't right in the first place,' he said.

'Maybe the brother will provide a quick and dirty solution.'

'Ah yes, Romeo. He's still our best bet.'

'There is also the possibility of a jealous husband or boyfriend,' Salter pointed out.

'Right. According to the Rundstedt woman, he was a bit of a ram when the right guest came along. That may be all bullshit, of course, in her own defence. She seems to have regarded him as attractive, but I have my doubts about how many would agree with her. According to the people here, there wasn't the slightest gossip on that score before. Still, he does seem to have thrown a leg over your compatriot.'

'She could be the only one. She seems to have trouble saying no to anyone.'

'So I gather. Anyway, there's nothing to be done until Miss America arrives.' Hamilton pulled all the documents together into a bundle and stuffed them into a drawer. 'Do you play squash?' he asked suddenly. 'I haven't had a game for two days because of this.'

Salter considered the question. He was at least ten years younger than Hamilton; he had been playing squash for more than a year, and he was holding his own among the middle-aged crowd at the Simcoe Squash Club.

'I don't have a racquet,' he said. 'And I'm not much good.'

Hamilton frowned and pulled the phone towards him. He dialled a number he found in his wallet. 'Derek,' he said. 'Got a court free? Eleven o'clock? Got an extra racquet there?' He put his hand over the receiver. 'Kit?' he asked Salter. Salter shook his head. 'Shoe size?' Hamilton asked. Salter told him. 'Got any extra togs, Derek? Shoe size nine. Good. We'll be along.' He put the phone down.

Three-quarters of an hour later and twenty miles away, Salter was being introduced to the custodian of a ramshackle wooden building in the middle of some sodden playing fields. 'Heart of England Police Athletic

Club,' Hamilton said.

They changed in a room more dilapidated than any Salter had seen outside Cabbagetown, the slum of his boyhood, with a corrugated iron cubicle at one end. 'The shower,' Hamilton said.

The court had been preserved intact since the Twenties, although the larger cracks had been recently filled in with cement.

Hamilton served. After three minutes, he said, 'You really aren't much good, are you?'

'I told you that,' Salter said.

'But you said you *played* the bloody game. All right. I'll give you a lesson. First. Hold your racquet like this. Now. *Hit* it.'

He instructed Salter for twenty minutes and then they had a little knock-up. Afterwards they washed themselves off in the trickle of tepid rusty water that came out of the iron pipe in the wall of the cubicle.

'Toronto is the squash capital of the world, I heard,' Hamilton said as they were driving back.

'I live in the suburbs,' Salter said. 'Do you play golf?'

Hamilton laughed. 'Got your goat, have I? No, I've been out, of course, but there's too much chat involved for me. Try Churcher.'

125

The two men were still together when the American girl arrived after lunch.

'Now, Miss Kryst,' Hamilton began. 'There was no need for you to come back. The local police could have taken a statement.'

'You think Mario killed Dillon, don't you? You're wrong. He wouldn't do anything like that. I came back to help him. He's not a killer, for God's sake. He's not.' She began to cry.

Hamilton leaned back in his chair. 'He's a witness, at least, and we can't find him,' he said. 'We thought you might be able to help. Nobody's in court yet.'

'But you think he's run away,' she cried. 'He hasn't anywhere to go. He can't work in England now that he's been fired by that dirty-minded swine.'

'Mr Dillon is dead,' Hamilton said.

'That doesn't change him.' She started to cry again.

'Where is Mario? He's not in Italy yet.'

'I don't know. He talked about finding some friends, getting some part-time work while he tried to get a new permit. Here. I've got a letter from him.' She held

126

out an envelope.

Hamilton took out the paper inside and raised his eyebrows.

'It's in Italian, of course,' the girl said. 'But all it says is that he will let me know when he has a permanent address, and some stuff about us.'

'Written yesterday,' Hamilton said.

'Yes. I got it this morning. He wouldn't be able to write that if he was frightened, would be?'

'No address.' Hamilton turned the letter over again. 'Postmarked Oxford. Thank you, Miss Kryst,' he said. 'That's all we need to know right now. Please enjoy the rest of your holiday.'

'I'm staying here,' she said. 'I'm going to see that Mario's all right.'

Hamilton raised his eyebrows again and looked around the office.

'If you need a place to say, Miss Kryst, my wife and I have found a good hotel,' Salter said.

'Who are you?'

'I was staying at Boomewood. I'm on holiday,' Salter said. 'Passing the time. Do you want me to phone?'

She nodded through her handkerchief, and

waited for Salter to telephone the Plough and confirm they had a room for her. Salter gave her directions. She ignored their goodbyes silently, putting away her handkerchief and buttoning her raincoat, keeping a determined distance from the two men.

When she had gone, Hamilton said, 'That's it, then, for the moment. What do you make of her?'

'She doesn't seem silly,' Salter said. 'And she sounds very sure of that waiter.'

'She's certainly going to a lot of trouble for him,' Hamilton agreed. 'Not everyone would want to get involved. But let's not piss about gossiping. Don't forget to have Mrs Nosey-Parker look over the register. What have you got on for this afternoon?'

'What time is it?'

'One-thirty.'

There was just time, he figured, to catch the last four races at Burford. 'I have to meet my wife,' he said. 'I'll drop by first thing in the morning.'

On the last race Salter decided to have a small bet on an outsider. Handing the bookie a twenty-pound note, he said, 'Two on Valerie's Choice.'

'Two tenners, Valerie's Choice,' the bookie called, and Salter let it stand.

Valerie's Choice won at ten to one and Salter, driving back to his hotel, reflected that there was nothing, absolutely nothing, quite as nice as a pocketful of money won by gambling.

At the hotel Salter found Maud drinking tea with Bonnie Kryst. She signalled him to stay away and he went upstairs to flush his betting slips down the toilet and tidy up. There was no sign of Annie, so he went downstairs again, where he found Maud now alone.

'Don't press her too hard, Maud,' Salter said when she had poured him a cup of tea. 'She's very upset.'

Maud looked at Salter for several moments. 'There's a bit more sensitivity in me than meets your eye, Charlie Salter. Or should I say ear. I haven't been pumping her, as you seem to think, but consoling her as best I can. Would you like to hear her story, as I got it?'

Salter nodded and put down a half-eaten chocolate cream biscuit, feeling a sudden longing for a butter tart.

'She's not in love with Mario, I think,'

Maud began, 'but she's his most loyal defender. This may be a bit subtle for a thick-skinned bobby, but I'll try and give it to you properly. Bonnie has been travelling around Europe for the past two months and she hasn't had a very good time. She was nearly raped in Paris— Paris was the worst, I gather. She said just walking along the street got her down because of the propositions— and in Munich, in a tram, a man put his hand up her skirt and wouldn't take it down until she screamed. Nobody came to her rescue. She was fondled in Stockholm, pinched in Brussels, and in Cannes an Arab taxi-driver exposed himself to her while she was trying to find the right change. She travels alone, you see, and she has that friendly air which must be the result of all that health food. Mind you, these things can happen to any of us. The creepy element just require that you be female.'

'It can happen in Boston, or New York, or Toronto if she walks slowly enough. Annie encountered a flasher on the Avenue Road bus last year,' Salter said, unimpressed.

'But European men seem to think that American girls are fair game. They assume that they have come over because they have heard of the prowess of the men here. They assume that a girl who travels alone is thus saying that she's available.'

'You don't think she's neurotic, then?'

'No, I don't. Now listen to the rest. The only country she had no trouble in was Italy, which I'd always heard was the worst.'

'There are lots of Italians in Boston. Maybe she knows how to read the signs with them. Besides, she speaks Italian.'

'Maybe. Whatever the reason, Bonnie loves Italy and all things Italian, and when she came to Boomewood her prejudices were confirmed.'

'By Mario?'

'By Mario. Take that look off your face and let me finish. Mario offered to show her London on his day off. She was wary, she says, but he gave her the nicest day she's had in the whole two months she's been here. They walked in Hyde Park, rode on sightseeing buses and ate fish and chips at Manzi's in Leicester Street. On the way home they stopped off at a pub and drank Amaretto.'

'Holding hands?'

'Probably, Charlie. What's that supposed to mean? Let me finish. The end of the story is the important bit. They went dutch all day, and she gave Mario her wallet so that she wouldn't have to carry a handbag. When they got back, he took her to her door and kissed her good night, thanking her for a lovely day. She says it was the nicest kiss she's ever had. And that was it. You see the point? She had laid down the ground rules in the morning and by the end of the day she was quite willing to change them, but he accepted them and stuck to them.'

'Maybe Mario's impotent,' Salter suggested.

'Oh, you prick, Charlie.'

'Sorry. So tell me about the wallet.'

'Yes, that's important. Next morning before breakfast Mario came to her room and she let him in so that no one would see them talking in the doorway. He had just come to bring back her wallet. Dillon saw him as he left the room and you know the rest.'

Salter waited. Then he asked. 'Why is this important, Maud?'

'Because if the girl is any judge at all, then Mario is no killer. It just isn't in him.'

'It wouldn't even convince a jury of romantics, Maud. She's hardly an unprejudiced character witness, is she? Do you believe it?'

'Yes, I do, Charlie. Nothing like that has ever happened to me, but I'm sure Mario is all right.'

'I'll tell them down at the station. They may laugh me out of the place, though. Now, they need your help.' He produced the Boomewood register. 'Look over the names of the people here, all the ones you saw around. Do you remember if any of them was in any way odd or unusual?'

Maud scanned the pages slowly. 'They've become a bit blurred now,' she said. 'No. Nothing.' She thumbed the pages back and forth, idly. 'I don't remember this one,' she said. 'A bit of an odd entry.' She turned the book around so that Salter could see. A week previously an entry appeared with a blank space between it and the previous entry, drawing attention to itself. There was no name, just 'Greetings from Valdottavo' scrawled in big letters. There was no address and no date.

'You remember someone from Italy?'

'No, I don't. But I don't remember some of the others, either, so maybe I was having an off day.'

Salter put a little tick by the entry. 'Okay,' he said. 'Let's have a drink. I'm sorry if I upset you, Maud. It's a nice story.'

Maud grimaced and stood up. 'You can make up for it by buying this old bag a gin and tonic. It's a bit early for Amaretto, or I'd have that.'

'Any sign of the brother?' he asked Hamilton next morning.

'Not yet. We'll catch him, though.'

In spite of himself, Salter had been impressed by Maud's conviction, and he told Hamilton the story as tonelessly as he could.

'What if he turns up with a knife in his boot?' Hamilton asked. But he too had listened to the story carefully.

Salter shrugged. He produced the Boomewood register. 'Maud Beresford was no help on this, I'm afraid. She couldn't remember anything strange about any of these people. She pointed this out, though.' He showed Hamilton the entry from Italy.

'Pity. I circulated Dillon's picture. We may turn up someone who knew him when he was underground. If we can fill in some of his past someone might come forward with a suggestion. In the meantime, let's go out to Boomewood. Maybe Mrs Dillon will have something more to tell us. She's calmed down now, but she is obviously terrified we'll find her brother.'

'What's her story now?'

'It's the same in the beginning. She went to *Romeo and Juliet* and got home sometime after midnight. She saw the light on in the office and went in and found Dillon stabbed on the floor. She was afraid immediately that it was her brother's doing and she panicked. She drove off to Oxford because she thought she knew where he might go— we checked it, he isn't there— and her idea was to protect him somehow, get him away, perhaps.'

'And the knife?'

'There was no knife that she remembers. She never touched one, anyway. Come and talk to her yourself.'

They were interrupted by Churcher. 'I thought you'd like to know, Charles, that we have found your Peeping Tom,' he said. 'Constable Dakin caught him last night outside the motel at the roundabout.'

'What's that?' Hamilton asked.

Salter explained. 'How do you know it's the same one?' he asked Churcher.

'Not much doubt, I think, when you see

him,' Churcher said, triumphant and mysterious. 'Shall I bring him in?'

Hamilton was looking amused. 'Certainly,' he said. 'Perhaps he'll tell us what he heard. Unless *Charles* would rather not.'

'Constable,' Churcher called. 'In here, please, with the accused.'

A uniformed constable entered, holding Gregory. But there was nothing left of the Smarmy Boy in the frightened youth looking for pity in the faces of the policemen around the room.

'I don't know what came over me,' he began immediately. 'I heard these people talking as I stopped for a minute and the constable, quite understandably, of course, got hold of me and brought me here.'

'What makes you think he was eavesdropping, Officer?' Hamilton said.

'He was in a state of acute sexual excitement, sir,' the constable said. ' 'Orrible little bleeder.'

'I was caught short, sir,' Gregory pleaded. 'I was having a slash.'

'Constable?'

'No, sir. He was enjoyin' 'isself.'

'All right. Leave us now, would you, Officer. Don't go far away in case this fiend gets out of control.' He bared his teeth at the pathetic Gregory. 'Have a chair, Churcher, while we interrogate him. It's your case.'

Churcher sat down, looking surprised and pleased. Gregory looked around for a chair for himself.

'Stand still, laddie,' Hamilton shouted. 'How old are you?'

'Eighteen, sir. Just turned.'

'Right. You're a man. You know the penalty for indecent exposure?'

'No, sir.'

'And trespass? And invasion of privacy?'

'No, sir.'

'You will be finished around here, laddie. Now, you also listened outside Mr Salter's window when he was staying at Boomewood, didn't you?'

'No, sir.'

'Yes, sir,' Hamilton corrected him. 'In fact you spent a lot of time listening around the bedrooms at Boomewood, didn't you?'

'No, sir.'

'Yes, sir,' Hamilton corrected him again. 'You heard a lot of things you'd like to tell us about, wouldn't you?'

'No, sir.'

'Yes, sir. I want you to think hard, laddie.

137

Because you may be in possession of vital evidence, vital to us, of whose significance you may not be aware. You have heard of turning Queen's evidence, have you? It means that in return for your cooperation we do our best to see that you get regarded favourably when your own case comes forward.'

Salter, in spite of feeling some pity for Gregory, nearly laughed. He could see the headlines, FLASHER TURNS INFORMER. He caught Hamilton's eye and composed himself.

'Right,' Hamilton said, when Gregory had had time to think. 'You did listen outside the bedroom windows at Boomewood, didn't you?'

'Sometimes I would hear things as I was passing on my way to bed, sir. My room was over the garage.'

'That's the idea. You did hear Mr Salter here one night, did you?'

'I heard something, sir, yes.'

'What?'

'Hey!' Salter protested.

Hamilton ignored him. 'I don't want to know the filthy details, laddie,' he continued. 'I just want to know if you could hear words. Don't tell me what they were.'

'More than that, sir.' Here Gregory looked at Salter. 'I heard the voice of another man in your room, sir.'

'You what!'

'Yes, sir. Another man with a funny accent, talking to someone called Nancy.'

Hamilton looked at Salter.

Salter said, 'Take my word for it, he heard right. I'll explain later, or maybe not. Go on.'

'All right, my boy, let's forget about the shenanigans in Mr Salter's room, and empty your mind of any other filth you may have heard, and tell us of anything, anything at all, that you heard which you think we should know about. Most of all about your former employer, Mr Dillon. Did you, in your travels, hear him in Miss Rundstedt's room?'

'Yes, sir.'

'I see. He made her his mistress while she was there, did he?'

'I don't know about that, sir. Mostly they seemed to talk and talk, and I couldn't hear much of what they were talking about but it didn't seem to be love talk, sir.'

Salter, who was beginning to get over his

139

early embarrassment, found himself blushing again, but no one was looking at him.

Gregory continued. 'And he wasn't the only one, sir, in her room. I heard her with another man one night and with him she *was* having it off.'

'Mario,' Hamilton said.

'No, sir. I'd have recognized Mario's voice. I didn't know this man but he wasn't Italian. English, I think.'

'A guest?'

'Not one I recognized, sir.'

'And you heard nothing else lately?'

'No, sir.'

'Think hard, laddie. The night before the row, when Mario got thrown out. Did you hear anything from any of the rooms?'

'You mean Miss Kryst's room, sir? No, I didn't. But they might have been very quiet. He was in her room next morning, wasn't he?'

'Was he? I understand he wasn't, at least not in a way to interest eavesdroppers. All right. Now I want you to look over this register. You waited at table in the mornings sometimes. Can you remember noticing anything unusual about any of these people? Or overhearing anything?'

Gregory looked carefully over the list of names. 'No, sir,' he said.

'What about this one,' Hamilton asked, pointing to the 'Valdottavo' entry. 'Do you remember any Italians recently?'

'No, sir. No one came from Italy lately that I know of.' It was obvious that Gregory was desperately eager to please Hamilton and scouring his memory for any scraps that would help, as he felt a tiny pulse of hope in Hamilton's manner. Although his face was still white, he was nearly in control of himself.

'All right, laddie. Inspector Churcher will deal with you. Off you go.'

The boy tried to smile at Hamilton and walked through the door. As Churcher got up to follow, Hamilton said, 'It's your case, Churcher, but I'd be pleased if you'd find some way of dealing with the brat without charging him. If he comes up before your local bench, old Beldin will be very hard on him. It won't help the boy.'

'It's a serious business, sir. A very nasty case,' Churcher protested.

'Yes, of course. But right now it's much more serious for him than it is for you. No one is laying a complaint against him, are you, Salter? I think it's our duty to help as well as punish, don't you, Inspector? Word will get around. They'll call him the Tokesbury Wanker. Isn't that enough?'

'Yes, sir. I'll inquire what counselling services are available to help people like him. Perhaps advise him to move.'

'Very wise, Churcher. Besides, if we keep him on a leash he may remember something else.'

The door closed. 'Let's go and have that chat with Mrs Dillon,' Hamilton said.

'Hang on a minute,' Salter said. 'Bring that kid back.'

When Churcher returned with Gregory, Salter said, 'This is important, Gregory. Nothing is missing, nothing is stolen, but I want to know if you ever went into the guests' bedrooms. Mine, for instance.'

'No, sir, never,' Gregory said promptly. 'Mr Dillon was very strict about that. He told us if he ever caught anyone except Mrs Peabody in any of the rooms he would give us the sack without any references. But I just remembered something else about you, sir. Mr Dillon knew you were a policeman. I heard him on the phone once mention the Toronto copper. That would be you, sir.'

'All right, laddie, off you go,' Hamilton said, and turned to stare interrogatively at Salter.

'Someone was in my room looking at my passport,' Salter said.

'Dillon?'

Salter shrugged. Hamilton brooded for a few moments, then picked up his coat off a chair beside the desk. It was an enormous, shapeless thing of many pockets that looked as if it was made out of tarpaulin. Hamilton saw Salter staring at it, and grinned. 'My wife claims I stole it off a dead poacher,' he said. 'Not true. I found it at Oxfam.'

Hamilton parked his car near the hotel and guided Salter into a coffee bar in the middle of the block opposite Boomewood. They joined a young workman who was reading a paper at a table by the window.

'Elevenses?' Hamilton asked the young man.

'That's right, sir. You don't often get a convenient spot for a cup of tea on these jobs. Usually I have to bring a Thermos flask.'

'So tell us what you've seen this morning.'

'Mrs Dillon is still in the hotel. No sign of

143

her this morning. But she's got a visitor. Girl arrived about half an hour ago, with luggage. That's her car across the street, illegally parked.'

'Bonnie Kryst,' Salter said.

'That's handy,' Hamilton said. 'Saves me a man.'

'Yes, sir. Hayes followed her here, of course. Then we tossed for it and he went off duty. He had to take his mum to the clinic, about her legs.'

'Okay, son. We're going over to have a little chat with Mrs Dillon now. We'll see you later.'

'Right you are, sir. While you're in there, could I pop round to the station and get a pullover? It's very cold on the corner there.'

'You can have fifteen minutes. All right?'

'Thank you, sir.'

Outside the coffee bar, Salter asked, 'You are keeping tabs on everybody?'

'I'm looking for Mario, Salter. I told you why I released Mrs Dillon. If Mario is our boy, there is a chance that he'll contact her or the Kryst girl— is already in touch with one of them. See?'

Salter wondered how much more was going on off-stage, and modified his impression that Hamilton was sitting in his office, waiting for something to happen.

The door was opened by Bonnie Kryst, who let the two policemen into the hall and waited for them to speak with the air of someone who now belonged at the hotel.

'We'd like your help, Miss Kryst,' Hamilton said. 'Mrs Dillon doesn't speak enough English and I need an interpreter.'

'Maria doesn't know where her brother is and nor do I,' Miss Kryst said, making no attempt to lead them further inside.

'I'm not here about her brother. I just want to ask Mrs Dillon some questions about the last few days.'

Bonnie Kryst turned away and walked down the hall into the kitchen. She returned in a few minutes and led them to where Mrs Dillon was sitting at a table, looking apprehensive. She spoke a few words of Italian to the American girl who replied soothingly.

'May we sit down?' Hamilton asked.

The girl translated, and when Mrs Dillon nodded she pointed to two chairs at the table, and sat down herself. Hamilton smiled at Mrs Dillon who was biting her nails compulsively and turned to the girl.

'First of all, Miss Kryst, I want to know if Mrs Dillon can tell us anything at all about her husband's life since 1944. It's a tall order, I know, but if we assume her brother is innocent – ' Hamilton paused at the word – 'then we have to assume that someone killed her husband for reasons we don't know about. We think he may have been expecting the man or woman who killed him, and that they talked for some time before Mr Dillon was killed. We know he was a deserter and that he managed without proper papers for thirty years, but what had he been doing?' Hamilton sat back and waited while the girl translated.

Mrs Dillon started shaking her head immediately and then spoke for some time. Bonnie Kryst translated. 'She only met him two years ago. He was in Valdottavo during the war – one or two of the older people remembered him being there. When he came back on a visit to Valdottavo he ate every day at the restaurant in Lucca where Maria worked and he began to court her. He went away for a little while, then returned and asked her to marry him and come to England. Except for her brother, she was all alone. Her husband was dead. So she accepted. He brought her here and they opened this place. Then he arranged for her little brother – ' here Bonnie Kryst blushed slightly – 'to come over to help out and to learn English. They were very happy until now. She wants to stay here, she says, but the police will probably not let her.'

'Tell her the police cannot stop her. She is a British citizen now.'

Mrs Dillon reacted to this news with another question.

'And her brother? Can he stay?'

'If he is not connected with this case, I think he can. I'll find out, but my guess is that Mrs Dillon can sponsor him as her husband did.'

Mrs Dillon stopped biting her nails and spoke rapidly and eagerly to Bonnie Kryst, who smiled and touched her shoulder.

They returned to Hamilton's original question. After a speech from Mrs Dillon, Bonnie Kryst said, 'She cannot remember if her husband ever mentioned any enemies. She doesn't know what he did before he turned up in Lucca. He told her he had been in business. She says he was a good man. There is a will leaving everything to her, and she is already a joint owner of the hotel. He was good to her brother, too, until this happened.'

Mrs Dillon spoke briefly and passionately. 'She says Dillon worshipped her and never looked at another woman. But lately he has gone a little crazy and she thought this Rundstedt woman must be the reason. She says Rundstedt must be a whore.'

'Why did he fire Mario?'

'She says her husband would not allow sleeping together in his hotel. Nobody who was not married could get a room together. He warned Mario when he arrived never to make passes at the female guests, and Mario never did. When Dillon saw Mario coming out of my room he lost his temper.'

Hamilton considered this. 'Try and find some way to put this delicately, Miss Kryst. I'd like to be absolutely sure that Dillon was not a womanizer. Did she or Mario ever suspect him before with any of the other guests?'

When this was translated, the Italian woman responded at length.

'Never,' Bonnie Kryst said. 'She says her husband loved her. That is why she thinks it is all Miss Rundstedt's fault.'

Mrs Dillon interjected at the mention of

148

Rundstedt's name. Bonnie Kryst looked puzzled and the two women worked on it for a few minutes, then Bonnie Kryst blushed. 'She says a woman like Miss Rundstedt has ways. That's more or less what she says.'

'Miss Kryst, even for a good man, Dillon's reaction was very violent. Had he ever shown any signs of such a temper before?'

Again the two women talked back and forth. 'She agrees,' Kryst said. 'It was strange and they were shocked by it. Mario thought he was a hypocrite, and he was not going to say anything but Dillon made him angry. Afterwards he told me he was sorry because it upset his sister.'

'He told you?'

'Yes. When he left. Frankly, Dillon sounds like a case of obsessional behaviour to me.'

'Yes? I never speculate about psychological forces, Miss Kryst. The theories behind them seem as crude as the theories of fifteenth-century medicine. However, you can see what I'm after. I'm trying to know something about this man, who he is, what he did for the thirty years for which we can find no trace of him, and what might have triggered him off lately, why his character suddenly changed, as they say. I'd like some concrete facts if I can get them. Were there any strangers around, any phone calls, letters, anything that he seemed to keep to himself? I have another question to ask and then I'll leave you to it. I don't want a final answer right now. Just talk to Mrs Dillon, would you, explain to her how important it is that we find some other possibility than her brother. I'll come back this afternoon for any trifles you've picked up. Now, here's my last question. Ask her to look over this register and see if it triggers her memory. Was there anything unusual about any of the guests?'

The girl translated, and Mrs Dillon hunched eagerly over the book. Almost immediately she put her finger on the entry from Valdottavo. She jumped up and went over to a drawer in the counter where she groped around at the back and came up with a picture postcard. It was a view of Lucca, in Tuscany. On the back was a message, 'Greetings from Valdottavo,' signed, 'Johnny'. It was postmarked 'Firenze'.

Bonnie Kryst said, 'This card came a month ago. Her husband threw it away, but later she found it in the back of this drawer. She asked her husband who Johnny was, but he said he didn't know. Then one day there was this entry in the register and no one knew how it had got there. It seemed to upset her husband, but it was soon forgotten. He said it must be a joke. Now she thinks her husband became strange from that time.'

'Let's not rush our fences, Miss Kryst. It probably was a joke that misfired. All right. Keep talking to her, would you, and I'll come back for any scraps you can gather.'

'Blackmail?' Salter asked, in the car.

'Possibly. Someone he didn't want to know turned up to tease him. But there was a meeting while the wife was at the theatre. A thousand pounds was made ready. Dillon's money? Now. You think there's anything to this gent from Italy?'

'If he exists he was in town a week ago. He didn't stay at Boomewood, but he might be listed in one of the other hotels.'

'We'll have a look, of course. Also—' Hamilton looked at the card in his pocket — 'Valdottavo. Maybe the local *gendarmerie* can turn something up for us round about the date that he sent this card.'

'*Carabinieri*,' Salter said.

'What?'

'*Carabinieri*. Not *gendarmerie.*'

'Really? What a lot you chaps know. Must come in very handy for doing crossword puzzles. Now I must get back to the office. Crime is breaking out all over. I'll send a message to Valdottavo, to the *Carabinieri*, and do the rounds of the hotels.' Hamilton pulled up outside the station. 'Well, Salter. I know you've been enjoying yourself, but I mustn't bugger up your holiday any more. Drop in tomorrow, if you like, and I'll tell you if anything has happened.' He nodded to the inspector to get out.

Just like that. Salter stood in the street feeling slightly foolish and cast adrift. At the same time he knew he had better take the opportunity to think about his vacation. The ever-soggy skies continued to leak or threaten, and their holiday had become stalled. On the whole, as Salter had pointed out, the Boomewood diversion had had its good side because he would not have remained cheerful on a steady diet of visiting abbeys in the rain, whereas Annie had found Maud (and occasionally Henry) ideal company for her kind of sightseeing. But it was time for him to make an effort.

The sergeant appeared at the station door

as if summoned, and Salter put his problem to him. 'Stratford,' the sergeant suggested. 'It's a bit of a drive, but you should make it for the first race. Freddie Tinsdale's got one going in the third. He always gets one ready for Stratford.'

Salter sighed. 'Won't do, Sergeant,' he said. 'But you've given me an idea.'

He bought a newspaper and looked up the theatre advertisements and made a phone call, securing four tickets for an evening performance at the theatre. The play was *The Taming of the Shrew* about which Salter knew nothing, but that hardly mattered; Annie would be pleased. He drove back to the Plough and laid his gift in front of the other three over beer and tongue sandwiches.

'How lovely,' Maud said immediately. 'I know Stratford a bit, but it would be nice to see it again. Dinner is on us, isn't it, Henry.' The thick lenses flashed with joy.

The rain was no more than a heavy mist as they set off after lunch. There being no market in progress when they arrived, they found a parking spot in the square and began looking at the preserved remains of Shakespeare's birthplace.

Salter found it impossible to feel what he was supposed to, and difficult to feel anything at first. As one of the hundreds of thousands of tourists who had trudged along this route, he was more conscious of the huge industry that Shakespeare had spawned than of any sense of reverence at the history that had soaked into these stones. He still retained a tiny but vivid awareness of bits of the one or two plays he had studied, but it was not enough to make this shrine speak to him immediately, and he felt untouched by the apparent religious awe of those around him. Missing any personal response, he determined to go without rather than simulate one.

They looked at Shakespeare's garden, his house, and several other significant buildings without any desire to linger on Salter's part. Then, in the church, which he had entered ahead of the others, he came unwarned to the famous inscription beginning, 'Good friend, for Jesus' sake forbear' and he felt the floor rock slightly as the voice of the man who had written those words spoke in his ear and made him slightly breathless. Then he wanted to go back and do the whole tour again, all by himself, but the others had

154

caught up with him and he let the moment go.

When they came out of the church, Salter looked at his watch. He made a show of patting his pockets worriedly and announced that his wallet was missing, he was sure that it was back in the car, that the others needn't trouble themselves, that he would just nip back and look, and he disappeared in the direction of the square where he had noticed a Turf Accountant's office. It was two minutes' work to look up the trainers in the third race, find Freddy Tinsdale's horse – something called Montague Road, and put five pounds on the nose. He trotted back to find the others, waving his wallet.

They ate a not-bad dinner in a frenchified restaurant and strolled along the river bank to the theatre, where Salter settled himself for a light doze, but he was disturbed before the curtain went up by a drunk three rows ahead of him who was terrorizing two nuns. The attendants seemed to be having trouble handling him, and Salter rose in his seat to help out, but Maud pulled him back and the drunk escaped and reappeared on stage where he pulled down all the scenery, at which everyone laughed, and Salter realized

155

he was one of the last in the audience to spot the drunk as a leading character in the production. Sharply awake now, he became engrossed in the play, and particularly enchanted with the costumes, which were not the bloomers and pantyhose he had been expecting, but the elegant suits and dark glasses of modern Italy. They set him brooding about the Italian connection in the Tokesbury Mallett murder.

At the end of the play, the transformation of Kate from shrew to broken-spirited spouse was so shocking that it silenced them all until they were in the car. Maud was the first to speak. 'He doesn't give one much choice, does he?'

'Who?' Henry said.

'Shakespeare. Was that play, or that production, I suppose I should say, an attack on women, on women's liberation, or what? I wish I could make up my mind.'

'That seems to give you a fair choice,' Henry said.

But no one else was inclined to talk about it yet. After a while, Salter, who had been thinking about his experiences in the church and the theatre, said, 'He's not dead, is he? I mean he really is still alive.'

He had made the journey all by himself, and no one pointed out to him that he was now one of all the other travellers who had made the same journey.

Montague Road won at thirteen to two and all Salter had to do the next morning was try to concoct an excuse to visit Stratford again and pick up his forty quid. I could bet my way round England, he thought.

They had to do some laundry, and Salter drove them in to Tokesbury Mallett and dropped in to the station house while Annie watched the machines spinning.

Churcher had his office back and was busily catching up on his work.

'There's nothing from the hotels,' he said, 'and we've heard nothing from Italy, either. No Englishman called Johnny has registered at a hotel near Valdottavo lately. That's a false lead. Superintendent Hamilton thinks it is probably a private joke between a couple of old buddies. At any rate it's a dead end, so we are concentrating on a blanket inquiry to see if we can find anything about Dillon's past. Long job, I'm afraid. I think the brother is probably our man, anyway. No sign of him yet and the longer he's missing, the more likely he's the one. I agree with the superintendent. He sends his regards, by the way, and best wishes for the rest of your holiday.'

Does he, indeed, thought Salter. Just like that? He could think of several things he would be doing himself, but he hesitated to make any suggestions. Hamilton knew his own business best. A more immediate concern was Churcher, who was being very cool, as who wouldn't be under the circumstances.

'I'm sorry we never took up that invitation to dinner, Charles,' he said. 'We'll be moving on almost immediately, I think, so I'll take a raincheck on it if I may.'

'You'll take a what?'

'I mean perhaps you'll invite me again if we come back.'

'Yes, of course. Now if you'll excuse me, I've got a lot on my plate this morning.'

Salter accepted the snub and left the station after a quick word of congratulation with the sergeant, and walked back to the laundromat. An idea was forming.

'Still raining,' he said to Annie.

'Let's push on, Charlie. The forecast for the Lake District is occasional showers. Even

158

that would be a change.'

'How long will we be here?' Salter indicated the dryer which Annie was now stuffing with clothes.

'Three-quarters of an hour.'

'I'll be right back.'

The travel agent was a Tweedledum and spent half an hour showing Salter how he could do what he wanted, and he returned to the laundromat armed with brochures and schedules.

'How would you like three days in Florence?' he asked, without preamble. 'Three days of sunshine and wine, and when we get back it might be spring.'

Annie sat down on the bench and stared at Salter. 'Why Florence?' she asked.

'Because the weather is good there right now, because you would enjoy it, and because I've found a package that will fly us there and give us a hotel and a car, from Birmingham.'

'Wow! Is it expensive?'

'It seems dirt cheap to me.'

'When?'

'Tomorrow morning.'

'Let me think.' But the idea caught her quickly, and she agreed in the car on the way

159

back to the Plough. At lunch they told the Beresfords, and suggested a little farewell dinner that night.

'I want to come,' Maud said.

'God Almighty,' Henry said. 'Look what you've done, Charlie. You've bewitched her. She thinks we're rich.'

The Salters were embarrassed. Money was not a major concern for them; Salter earned a huge salary by English standards, and Annie had her own trust fund, as well as her income from her job. They were aware, however, that the Beresfords might be on a tighter budget, and they were uncomfortable in the role of rich Americans.

Annie said, 'We can't drag you away from your holiday, just to keep us company. We'll be all right.'

Maud said, 'I want to come.'

'We can go if you want to,' Henry said. 'I'll sell the house when we get back.' Then, more gracefully, 'No, really, if you'll have us, it's probably the ideal opportunity. Maud has always wanted to go.'

Annie said, 'It would be nice to have you along, Maud. Charlie won't go into an art gallery. Can you imagine being in Florence and not seeing the Uffizi?'

'It's not that I don't like pictures,' Salter said. 'I'll come with you to see the Mona Lisa . . .'

'That's in Paris.'

'Well, one picture of your choice, then. It's the bloody galleries themselves. You are always viewing the remains in a whisper. If you try to talk normally they kick you out.'

'If I'm going to spend my inheritance on going to Florence, I want to see some pictures,' Henry said.

'I'll be all right,' Salter said. 'I'll just have a mooch round, looking at the beggars and whores.'

'Let's go, Henry,' Maud pleaded.

And so it was arranged. Salter and Annie conferred privately, and concocted a plan whereby he would buy two packages, one for the Beresfords and one for themselves in which they would bear the full cost of the car alone, and Salter drove into Tokesbury Mallett to arrange it. The agent enjoyed the little conspiracy and marked up the tickets so that it would not be obvious to the Beresfords that they were paying less, and Salter went off to the bank to get some lire. When he returned to the agent, he bumped into a slightly familiar figure on his way out. As

161

the man went to step away from him, Salter remembered who he was. Hamilton's assistant. 'Sergeant Woodiwiss,' he said. 'How's it going?'

'Oh yes. Inspector Salter, isn't it?' He jerked his head at the agency. 'Moving on, are you?'

'Just wanted to see what they have to offer,' Salter said. 'Sightseeing buses, that sort of thing. What about you?'

'Just thinking about my holidays, sir. Somewhere dry.'

'Made any progess?' Salter asked.

'How do you mean, sir?' Woodiwiss countered, his face bland.

Cagey bastard, thought Salter. 'With your holiday plans,' he said. 'Give your superintendent my regards,' he added.

'I'll do that, sir,' Woodiwiss said and walked away.

Inside, Salter put his money on the counter, and collected his tickets. 'Everybody's travelling today, it seems,' he said. 'I just bumped into a friend of mine in the doorway. Where's he off to?'

'The gentleman in the raincoat?' the agent said. 'He was just inquiring.' He walked back to his desk behind the counter.

'Will the car be waiting for me at Pisa?' Salter asked.

'It's all on the ticket,' the agent said without looking up, turning into a Tweedledee in front of Salter's eyes.

Three

Interlude in Florence

At Pisa they stepped out of the aircraft into
the Italian spring. Underneath the smell of
kerosene was a richer, older scent that told
them they were no longer in England, the
smell of a sun-soaked world compounded of
unfamiliar flora, a fragrance sweeter and
heavier than that of the English countryside.
They picked up the car and turned on to the
autostrada.

'It's all true,' Annie said.

'What?' asked Henry.

'Italy. Look at it.' She waved her hand at
the golden landscape. 'I thought this light
was an invention of Renaissance painters,
something to do with the olive oil they
mixed their paints with. I didn't think the
world could really be that colour here. And
look at those trees. I thought Italian painters
had a passion for painting trees in rows, but

it is like that. Look at those forests – are they forests? And those trees lining the roads – they look as if they were put in by a giant machine. What are they?'

'Cypresses, I think,' Maud said. 'That's what you always hear about, anyway.'

'There's no grass,' Annie said suddenly. 'All the houses are surrounded by gravel.'

'That's one of the things you can't smell,' Salter said authoritatively. 'Most people don't realize that grass smells. Not hay – grass. I spent six months in the Arctic once. When I came out, the smell of grass was the first thing that hit me in the Winnipeg airport.'

'Six months in the Arctic, Charlie? That's *very* impressive. Did you have to eat your dogs, that sort of thing?'

Before Salter could decide if Maud was making fun of him – had he told too many stories about life in the Canadian bush? – Annie interrupted. 'Look,' she said, pointing to a village on the top of a hill like a crown of brick. 'That *is* a painting, isn't it?'

'I think all the paintings have one of those,' Henry said.

Salter drove on at a hundred and twenty kilometres an hour, happy to be on the right side of the road again, undisturbed that everything on the highway passed him as if he were jogging.

They reached the outskirts of Florence in the afternoon and put aside Italy for an hour while they found a place to park. Salter offered the wheel to anyone who wanted to drive, and when his offer was refused, announced that he was going to enjoy himself. 'I'm going to drive round and round in circles,' he said. 'Without advice or help from anyone. We know the hotel is somewhere in the middle of Florence and we can walk from wherever I find a spot. I want no one to point out that we just missed a place. When *I* see a spot which *I* think I can get into, I'll take it. Now enjoy the sights.'

Annie poked her tongue out at him and Henry looked triumphantly at Maud, who sneered back, but everyone stayed gagged until Salter parked at the Piazza Indipendenza within two blocks of the hotel. Salter led the way into the lobby, where a young man sat behind the desk.

'*Deux camera matrimoniales pour Salter und Beresford,*' Salter said, getting four languages into the seven words.

'Could I see your passports, please?' the

166

young man said after a few moments. Then: 'Ah yes, we have your reservations. This way, please.'

The tiled rooms were big and sunny with wooden shutters that opened on to balaconies overlooking the tiny street below. No one wanted to linger and they dumped their bags and wandered out, content to follow their noses into the crowds.

'The shops here are open until eight,' Maud sighed, as they shuffled happily along, pricing the clothes and looking for a restaurant. They had coffee at this café, followed by wine at that one.

'No wonder they came here,' Maud said.

'Who?' Henry asked.

'Byron, Shelley, Keats, Browning,' Maud said. 'Everybody.'

They ate dinner in a restaurant that looked affordable and where the food was nearly as good as that at Boomewood.

'Some people get to honeymoon here,' Maud said. 'We went to Yarmouth, didn't we, Henry?'

They drank two litres of wine with the food; then, overcome, they walked back to the hotel and to bed.

'What do you want to do here, Charlie?' Annie asked, after they had showered and were lying clean and cool on top of the bed.

For answer, Salter traced a route which began at her left ear, took in most of the country below, and ended at her other ear. Annie responded by turning on her stomach and running a smoothing hand over his chest. 'For three days, I mean,' she said.

This was a more delicate question. 'I'd like to see a bit of the country,' he said. 'We have a car.'

'Like where?'

'I thought I'd like to take a look at the village Dillon lived in during the war.'

'Once a copper, always a copper, eh?' She laid her head on his stomach and looked at him over his chest.

'All right,' he agreed. 'So I'm curious about this case. As far as I know, all Hamilton's done is phone to see if anyone called Johnny was around Valdottavo lately. A message like that gets in someone's IN tray, he makes three phone calls, marks it NO TRACE and puts it in the OUT-tray. I'd like to look for myself. According to Churcher, the English are now betting on Mario, but there's too much other stuff.

Apart from this Johnny, I mean. Who was looking at my passport? Who was playing at "wakey-wakey"? What was Dillon doing with a thousand pounds in an envelope? Last of all, why does a guy like Dillon suddenly spend a night with the Rundstedt woman? According to Gregory, all they did was talk and you can trust him on that.'

'You're assuming Mario didn't do it?'

'I'm not assuming anything. But the story Maud got out of Bonnie Kryst sounded pretty good to me. If I were Hamilton I'd be looking a lot harder in a lot of places.'

'Do you think this superintendent is a fool?'

'No, I don't. That's why I can't understand why there's not more activity.'

'What's the motive, Charlie?'

'How the hell do I know? Money, blackmail, something like that.'

'Not the killer's. Yours.'

'Me? I'm just curious.'

Annie tweaked a hair on his chest. 'You know what I think?' she said. 'I think you're just mad because he beat you so easily at squash.'

'What! That's ridiculous, for Christ's sake. I told you, I'm curious, that's all.'

169

'So what are you going to do?'

'I thought I'd drive out to this Valdottavo place and poke around until I found someone who knew Dillon during the war. And dig a little deeper for this Johnny. You'll be okay here with Maud, won't you?'

Annie rolled off him and stretched herself by his side. 'Why don't I come along?' she said.

'Oh no. Enjoy your holiday. Stay here and look at Florence.'

'I *am* enjoying my holiday. We are only going to get a taste of the country in three days, anyway, so it doesn't matter what we do. We'll be back. But you need an interpreter. You just speak Canajun and ten words of French. At least I can understand some of what's being said to me by sorting through my French and Latin.'

Salter considered this. It was true that within half an hour of arriving Annie and Maud had created a technique for communicating with waiters by making the waiters speak very slowly and choosing items they recognized as they moved through the menu. The technique also worked in shops, but it required an elementary background in another language than English. On his own,

Salter was dumb. 'You wouldn't mind?' he asked.

'It might be fun. I've never seen you on the job before.'

'Okay. But don't tell Maud what we are up to, will you? She'll want to come, too.'

'No problem. I'll tell her we'd like a day by ourselves.'

'Terrific,' Salter said. He turned on his elbow. 'Did I ever tell you thy belly was like an heap of wheat?' he asked.

'Yes, but not since we left Canada.'

'No? I guess you need a warm climate so you can see it.'

'Right,' Maud said, taking charge at breakfast next day. 'What are our priorities? We have three days.'

'I want to see some pictures,' Henry said.

'I wouldn't mind doing a bit of shopping,' Maud said. 'But that can wait. Charlie wants to see some beggars and whores. What about you, Annie?'

'I'd also like to see a bit of the country,' Salter said. 'We have a car.'

Annie's move.

'Maybe we should split up for the day,' she said. 'Charlie and I will go for a ride, then you two could go off tomorrow. If the four of us stay together all the time we'll get on each other's nerves.'

A tiny chill passed over the table while the Beresfords considered the implications of this. Then Maud said, 'Very sensible, Annie. There speaks the experienced world traveller. But you'll have to come shopping with me at some point. After today I'll need a rest from Henry, too, won't I, dear? See you here for dinner, then. About six?'

After Maud and Henry had left, Salter pored over his map while they drank some more coffee. Their route lay first along the autostrada to Viareggio. From Lucca they would take the road to Ponte a Moriano, across a small bridge and on up to Valdottavo. With luck they should be able to do most of it in the morning and come back by a different route in the afternoon.

Leaving Florence was easy. They found the autostrada to Viareggio and forty-five minutes later were circling the walled town of Lucca. They circled Lucca three times before a policeman put them on the right road, and after that they began to see signs for Ponte a Moriano. Salter had little idea how he intended to proceed, and no idea at all of what he was looking for, but it was a superb day and all things considered he was just as happy to be driving around Italy in the sun as England in the rain. He pulled up at a café in Ponte a Moriano where Annie got some more directions by pointing at Valdottavo on the map, learning to her pleasure that in Italian the word for 'left' is '*sinistra*'.

As they approached Valdottavo, Salter saw a sign for '*Carabinieri*' and a problem occurred to him. 'If I check with the police,' he said, 'they might get curious, especially if Hamilton has already asked them to check.'

'Stop at that café,' Annie said. 'We'll just ask around. You see what a help I am? We look like a couple of Americans inquiring after an old friend. Much better than if you were on your own, reeking of the man from headquarters.'

Salter parked the car and they walked into the café. There were only three tables inside and at one of them four old men were playing cards. They ordered some *vino bianco*, for which they were charged twenty-three cents a glass, and sat considering how best to proceed. Then Annie wrote out the name

'Terry Dillon' on a scrap of paper and Salter signalled the owner for more wine. When he brought the bottle to their table, Annie showed him the name and said slowly, 'We are searching for this man, Terry Dillon.' She had thought about her words carefully, and chosen a verb that sounded similar in French as being likely to have an Italian cognate, but the barman shook his head and smiled.

'Looking for,' Annie said. 'Seeking, desiring,' and finally 'losing', adding the name Terry Dillon after each verb choice.

Still the man shook his head. *'Tedeschi?'* he asked.

Annie shook her head. *'Inglesi,'* she said. Was that Spanish? 'Canada,' she added.

It worked. The barman looked knowing, then walked over to the four old men and spoke briefly to one of them, who nodded and accompanied the barman to the Salters' table, where he sat down and waited for them to speak.

'We are looking for, searching, seeking, not finding, this man,' Annie said, not sure what the old man's role was.

The Italian smiled. 'I hope you find him,' he said.

'You speak English?' Salter asked in relief. The man nodded. 'I was a prisoner of war for three years on a farm in Cheddar, in England,' he said. 'What do you want to know?'

At the other table the three remaining card-players were smiling and pointing, taking pleasure in the skill of the village linguist.

'I am trying to find someone who knew this man,' Salter said. 'He lived here a long time ago,' he added, instinctively slipping into the simple language of folk tales.

'My name is Franco,' the man said, and offered his hand, making Salter and Annie feel slightly discourteous for not having observed the formalities first. He looked at the name and shook his head, then walked over and showed it to the other players. The three men passed the paper around and shook their heads.

Salter tried another tack. 'This man, Terry Dillon, married a woman from Lucca a few years ago, maybe just two years. Maria Ponti. She went with him to England, and her brother Mario went with her this year.'

Franco translated this and the old men exploded in recognition. 'We know him,'

Franco said. 'This man Terry Dillon was here in the war, yes? He came back and married the woman from Lucca.'

'That's right. Does anyone know anything about him?'

The men talked among themselves, then Franco stood up. 'Let's go to the trattoria. We think the owner knew him.'

They all left the café and walked about two hundred yards down the street, then turned off into the front yard of the trattoria. The owner was standing in the doorway and Franco spoke to him, telling him Salter's story. The man shook hands with the Salters and pointed to a large table under a tree where everybody sat down while he collected a huge flask of wine and some glasses from the bar. When he had filled their glasses he began to talk. Periodically one of the card-players would add something, and there would be an exchange among the group as the details of the story were confirmed. When the owner was finished, Franco started the translation.

'Here is the story,' he said. 'During the war there were these two Englishmen— Tommies— Terry Dillon and another one— who got lost behind the German lines. We found them – the people in Valdottavo – and a man named Giovanni Carosio hid them on his farm. They worked for him and he kept them away from the Germans. This was easy at first, but when the war went bad for us the Fascisti were looking for more young men for the army. They were looking for Italians hiding from the war. Some rich families in Rome and Florence paid farmers to keep their sons hidden from the war. The Fascisti were looking for these and Giovanni knew he could not hide the Englishmen any more so he sent them away. No one saw them again, until, like you said, Terry Dillon came back about two years ago.'

'What happened to the other one?'

Franco directed the question to the owner and repeated it around the group, but no one responded except to shake their heads. 'They don't know. Nobody here knew the English-men – we were all in the army – but every-one knows this story.'

'What about Giovanni Carosio? Would he know?'

'Sure, but he's dead. But we can ask his daughter.' He stood up. 'She was only a child during the war but she will know the story.'

Salter's offer to pay for the wine was refused, and once more the group assembled in the road.

'You have a car?' Franco asked. 'Let's use that.'

They walked back to the café where Salter and Annie shook hands with the three other card-players, and Franco climbed into the front seat. He directed Salter through the village and up a winding road, then off to a gravel track which took them to the top of a hill overlooking the village. Whatever I find out, thought Salter, I'm certainly seeing the country.

The track ended at a two-storey brick-and-stone farmhouse surrounded by fruit trees. In front, a fair-haired woman in her forties was seated at a wooden table under a vine-leaf arbour, sorting over a mound of beans. She greeted Franco, bantering with him briefly, and shook hands with the Salters as Franco introduced them. She invited everyone to sit down and produced some wine, and Franco told her Salter's story. Before he had gone very far, she was nodding and smiling in confirmation. Then she told Franco her version.

'Signor Dillon came back to see her father,

178

to thank him for looking after him during the war,' Franco translated.

'After thirty-five years?' Salter asked.

Franco translated. The woman nodded and spoke. 'She says Signor Dillon told her that he was retired now and could afford to travel,' Franco said.

'Okay. What else?'

'She says Dillon told her that when the two Tommies had to leave the farm they hid in the woods up there.' Franco waved at the hills in the distance. 'Then they met some English paratroopers who gave them money and weapons and told them to make their way south. The armies were all mixed up and if they were careful they could slip through and get to their own soldiers. That's what Terry Dillon did.'

'And the other one?'

'Johnny?' the woman asked, and spoke a few words.

'Johnny is dead,' Franco translated.

'Dead?'

'Yes. Dillon said he was killed in the woods,' the translation continued.

'Was Dillon with him?'

The woman shrugged and spoke briefly.

'She doesn't know,' Franco said.

'So he might have escaped,' Salter said. He explained about the postcard from Valdottavo. 'It must be the same person,' he concluded.

Franco translated, and the woman shook her head decisively and spoke at length.

'No,' Franco said. 'If Johnny came back she would know. He used to play with her when she was a little girl. He would come to see her. Johnny never came back.'

The woman exclaimed and ran into the house. She returned with a photograph, an old snapshot of two Tommies with their arms around each other's shoulders. There was nothing distinctive about the two soldiers; the picture had been taken in England, and in the back garden of a small house: two eighteen-year-olds in battledress with cheerful grins that showed they had both lost some teeth to the army dentist. The real English disease.

'Which is which?' Salter asked.

The woman turned the picture over and showed him the back. An inscription read, 'Blighty, 1942. Johnny and Terry.' She turned the picture over again and pointed. 'Terry Dillon; Johnny Bessell.' She laughed and said something more. 'When Terry Dillon came back he was fat with a big grey beard,' Franco translated. 'She did not recognize him.'

'I know,' Salter said. 'I met him in England.' He decided not to spoil her day by telling her of Dillon's death. 'Thank her for me, please, Franco.'

They shook hands again all round, and Annie said, *'Arrivederci,'* to everyone's enormous pleasure, and Salter drove Franco back to the café where he had first found him. Once more they shook hands, but Franco made no move to get out of the car. Then he said, 'Signor Salter, everyone is asking me who you are, so now I will ask you. Why is a Canadian looking for an Englishman who lived in Italy in the war? Something bad?'

It was a question Salter had expected much earlier, but he still didn't have a reply. Annie filled the gap. 'It's about some money,' she said. 'A relative of Johnny Bessell died in Canada and left some money to him. But he has not claimed the money so my husband is trying to prove he is dead.'

Franco looked at Annie, then at Salter. 'You are a lawyer?' he asked.

'Sort of,' Salter said. 'I trace missing people.'

'You will spend all his money looking for him,' Franco said. Then he shrugged. 'There is one other place you can ask,' he said. 'The post office. The girl there speaks English, too. Good luck.'

They drove off in the direction Franco had indicated, and Salter pulled up outside the post office.

'Franco didn't believe me,' he said to Annie.

'No, he didn't,' she agreed. 'I'm not surprised. Why did you tell him you had met Dillon in England?'

'Oh Christ, I said that, didn't I? What do you think they'll make of us?'

'Nothing probably. They'll think this Johnny Bessell will be a millionaire if we find him, and talk about it for a few days. Come on, let's get this girl in the Post Office done with. I'm slightly drunk and famished.'

The girl who ran the post office knew all about Signor Dillon and confirmed the story that Salter already knew. She said that no one called Bessell had received any mail there; she was quite positive because it was still early in the season and there were very few foreigners yet. 'But why is everyone interested in Signor Dillon?' she added.

'Everyone? Who else?'

'Another man last month. He knew the story of the two Tommies in the war, too, and he was looking for Signor Dillon. He did not go into the village, after I told him that Signor Dillon was in England.'

'Do you remember what he looked like?'

'Not really. English, I think. Older than you. He was just in for a few minutes. I told him he could probably get Signor Dillon's English address from the trattoria in Lucca where his wife worked.'

Salter thanked her, watching to see if this was another time to shake hands, but she merely smiled and went back to work.

'So Bessell's been here,' he said to Annie on their way to Lucca. 'It had to be him. But why incognito? Why didn't he go up to the village and say hello?'

'Because he wanted to give Dillon a surprise,' Annie said.

'Catch him by surprise, you mean?'

Annie shrugged. 'What next?' she asked. 'Do you ever eat when you are on a case?'

They were approaching the walled town

again. 'Let's see if they sell lunch in Lucca,' Salter said.

They parked by a gate in the wall and strolled into the town, coming quickly upon what they wanted, a restaurant at the corner of a large square with plenty of room at the tables outside. After an enormous meal that cost them twenty dollars, including, apparently, seventy-five cents for a bottle of wine that Salter calculated would have cost him nine times as much in an Ontario liquor store, and twenty times as much in the neighbourhood restaurant he and Annie favoured because it was cheap, Salter decided he had a problem.

'I need a siesta,' he said.

Annie laughed. 'You're drunk,' she said.

'Content,' Salter said. 'Just content. Anyway, when in Rome . . .'

They watched in silence as the shops began to close for the afternoon.

'Got any suggestions?' Annie asked. 'I could do with a nap, too.'

'If we were at home, now — travelling, I mean — we would find ourselves a bit of grass by the highway, but they don't seem to do that here. Maybe the risk of *banditti* is too great.'

Annie said, 'All the stories you hear about Rome and Naples, about how people are always getting robbed. Nobody's even tried to short-change us yet.'

It was true. They had found restaurant bills impossible to read, which should have made them nervous, but the total was always so small that they couldn't believe anyone was cheating. The experience they had had so far was that it was impossible to eat badly in Italy and all meals cost ten dollars. Bread seemed to cost a dollar a head and wine seventy-five cents, and whatever else they ate cost six or seven dollars.

'Nobody cheats on bills at home, either,' Salter said loyally.

'Only the very expensive restaurants downtown,' Annie corrected, her eyes closed. The pauses between their remarks were becoming longer.

'You remember that first hotel in England?' Salter said, minutes later.

'Tweedledee,' Annie said.

They were very nearly asleep. They woke up to a mild squabble a few tables away between a waiter and a middle-aged English couple. They turned their chairs slightly, the better to listen and watch in comfort. The

185

English couple were questioning an item on their bill, determined not to be robbed by foreigners. Salter admired their courage and predicted to himself that they were about to be embarrassed. Eventually the baffled waiter called the manager who spoke some English and pointed out that the item they had never ordered and were refusing to pay for was the date. The couple left, pink-faced, staring high over the heads of their audience.

Salter and Annie, slightly energized, resumed their conversation.

'In Florida once we rented a motel for a couple of hours, remember?'

'I remember. I felt like your secretary.'

'You think we might get a room here for the afternoon?'

'Sure, if you know what to ask for. Go ahead. I'll wait in the car.

'What's the Italian for "hours"?'

'I don't know. The Latin is *"hora"*, I think.'

Salter tried out a sentence. *'Uno camera matrimoniale Pour duo hora,'* he said.

'I'd check that if I were you,' Annie said. 'You might wind up in a room with me and two other ladies. Cost you a fortune.'

'For all I know we'll wind up in jail,'

Salter said. 'Who knows what the local laws are. Maybe it's illegal not to stay overnight.'

'You aren't going to risk it, are you?' Annie said.

'No. All I want is a nap. If we got a room covered in red velvet with a mirror on the ceiling it would keep me awake.'

By now they were alone at the tables outside the café. 'Let's go back to the car, Charlie, and take it from there,' Annie said.

They shambled, jelly-like, through the nearly empty streets of the town to the car parked outside the gate. Here Salter moved the car into the shade where it could be seen by a policeman on traffic duty twenty yards away. They rolled the windows down slightly, adjusted the seats back as far as they would go, and passed out.

When they woke up, thick-tongued and disoriented, they needed coffee before tackling the autostrada to Florence, and they walked back into the town. Annie bought a guide-book, and they became tourists for an hour, paying a visit to the Roman amphitheatre where the first boutiques were peeping through the otherwise scruffy arena, the universal sign of urban renewal. When they got their coffee, the waiter told them they should stay until Sunday; an election was coming up and the local Communist candidate, a lady, had promised to campaign in the nude.

They drove back to the Piazza Indipendenza in plenty of time for dinner, and waited for the others to appear.

Maud and Henry had spent most of the day in the Uffizi Galleries, and like the Salters, they had found a siesta irresistible.

'What did you do?' Maud asked.

They told the Beresfords how they had driven around the Tuscan hills, had lunch at this wonderful town called Lucca, and poked about the streets in the afternoon. Annie suggested that Maud and Henry take a similar route the next day, but Henry declined. 'I don't trust myself on the wrong side of the road,' he said, 'so to avoid arguments I left my licence at home.'

Salter offered to chauffeur them, but Maud turned it down. 'We want some more culture,' she said. 'Henry is insatiable.' So they agreed that they would do the Pitti Palace, the Boboli Gardens, and take another look (at Henry's request) at the Uffizi Galleries.

The whole of the next day they looked and

walked, with a two-hour break for a siesta. Salter, remembering his Stratford experience, went with the flow, prepared to be untouched unless something snagged him. He was indifferent to the Duomo and found the formality of the Boboli Gardens bleak after England. Although nothing spoke to him like Shakespeare's inscription, he nearly lost himself once at the sight of the restored original of a painting he knew as Venus on the Half-Shell, a poster of which Annie had owned when he married her. The hermit in him was struck, too, by the cells of the monks in the Museum of San Marco, especially that of Savonarola. Apart from all the praying, he thought, looking around the pleasant rooms, it wouldn't be a bad life – wine with every meal, a good dressing-gown to keep you warm, and all the time in this world to read and think. A life of total selfishness, apart from the praying.

During dinner they re-sorted their priorities for their last day.

'I've had enough culture,' Salter said. 'I want to see the rest of the town.'

'I haven't seen the Palazzo Vecchio yet,' Henry said.

'You've got to come shopping with me,

Annie,' Maud said.

So they planned the morning. They would meet for lunch, and take the rest of the day from there, probably after a sleep.

In bed Annie said, 'Got an idea, have you, Charlie?'

'Nothing much,' Salter said. 'I just wondered if I could find out if Bessell was officially buried up in those hills. There must be some sort of War Graves Commission.'

'Then what?'

'Then nothing,' Salter said. 'Then I'll tell Churcher what I've found out, and he can tell Hamilton. Give Churcher a bit of a boost.'

'A bit risky, isn't it? If Hamilton gets irritated because you've found out something he ought to have done, it will backfire on Churcher, won't it?'

Salter considered. 'Yeah, you're right. I'll leave him out of it. If I can find out that Johnny Bessell is still alive, or anyway not certainly dead, I'll tell Hamilton. Maybe it will upset him.' Salter smiled.

'Charlie,' Annie said, 'you aren't going to spend the rest of the holiday on this, are you?'

'Of course not. I'm not bothering anyone, am I?'

'No. Even better than that. I'm glad you found out about steeplechasing because you would have been a bloody misery otherwise. Maud and I have had a good time without you. And this murder has kept you cheerful the rest of the time. So I'm not complaining. And, too, I have to thank the policeman in you for Florence, which you might not have suggested all by yourself. So we've all had a good time where we might have been getting on each other's nerves by now. And I did enjoy the bit of sleuthing in Valdottavo. But when we go back, I want to carry on with the holiday as planned, especially if the sun has come out.'

'There's nothing else to do, anyway. Don't worry about it. But while we are on the subject, will you come with me to the races?'

'Sure. I'd love to. But not in the pouring rain.'

'I'll buy a one-day pass to the Members' Enclosure,' Salter said. 'We'll watch with the gentry. I'll buy one of those flat hats they all wear and a pair of those green boots.'

It took Salter most of the morning to find

out what he wanted to know. He was tempted to identify himself properly, but while that might have produced quicker results, it was certain to lead to some polite questions that he didn't want to answer, and maybe an exchange of pleasantries between the *carabinieri* and Hamilton. So he played the friend of a friend, inquiring on his behalf about an old army buddy, and after bumping around various police and army offices, feeling more and more ashamed of his Anglo-Saxon monolingualism (why the bloody hell didn't they at least teach us some French in Ontario? — all these Italian coppers seemed to speak at least one other language) he was referred to the British Consul, where he was shown a list and found no trace of Johnny Bessell.

As with the trip to Valdottavo, having an errand got him into the city in a way that merely strolling around it as a tourist would not have done. He saw no beggars, but a beautiful girl spoke invitingly to him near the Pitti Palace which could only mean one thing, and he had a nice encounter with an English-speaking waiter who was thrilled to learn that Salter came from Toronto, where the waiter's hero was now playing soccer for the Blizzard. A good mooch round.

After lunch and a short nap, the four of them discussed how to get the best out of their last few hours. Henry, predictably, wanted to do two more museums and a church, and when Maud refused, Annie offered to accompany him, which left Maud and Salter.

'I wouldn't mind doing some shopping,' Salter said. 'When *she's* around trying to get me to buy stuff for myself, I get Bolshie.'

'Don't I know it,' Annie said. 'Let's split up, then. What about you, Maud?'

'I'll go with Charlie,' Maud said. 'I'll make him spend his money.'

They started in the leather market, where Salter bought a belt for himself and a purse for Annie which Maud said Annie had admired but her Scottish ancestors thought too expensive. Then they made their way to the Ponte Vecchio to look at gold. Near the straw market they stopped at a café where Salter had his first beer in three days, and Maud ordered a huge glass, like a vase, of fruit and wine. The holiday was nearly over.

'How it infects the blood!' Maud said.

'What?' Salter asked.

For reply, Maud pointed to a young couple who had stopped in a doorway so that the boy could kiss the girl's eyes and neck and ears. 'Italy,' Maud said.

'What a great holiday,' Salter said. He meant what an agreeable companion Maud had turned out to be, what a difference from his first impression of her as a myopic busybody, and he tried to put all this into his voice. Maud, who was still watching the boy and girl, said, 'Have you ever had an affair, Charlie? Since you were married, I mean?'

Salter looked at her warily. She had taken off her glasses, and without them she had a slightly mad look.

'You want to know too much, Maud,' he said.

'Don't I, though.'

'Do your eyes hurt?' Salter asked.

'No. It's just easier to talk abnormally without my glasses on. Have you?'

Salter found himself caught among the desire to brag (I've had more affairs than you've had hot dinners), the desire to invent a virtuous persona (I respect Annie too much for that, Maud), and the truth. But any answer would involve, with Maud, a further discussion of why, or why not. He prevaricated.

'Are you making a pass at me, Maud?' he joked.

'No, I'm not. I just wondered about other people's lifestyles, as you call it.'

Salter had the initiative now, and he tried to deflect attention from himself. 'What about you, Maud? Are you and Henry involved in a wife-swapping ring in Watford?'

'Don't be vulgar, Charlie. That's not what I meant.'

'Sorry. But have you, Maud? Ever been unfaithful?'

'Yes, I have,' Maud said promptly. 'Once. With an old boyfriend I knew before I married Henry. I met him again years later and we went to bed. We never had before.'

'And?'

'It was bloody alarming. I kept expecting photographers to burst in.'

Salter laughed. 'Why did you do it, then?'

'I was curious. I wanted to know if I'd missed anything.'

'Not a *real* affair, then.'

'No. When I put my glasses back on he had a smug expression on his face, and I realized that he thought he had shown me what I had missed, or was doing me a favour because I was frustrated. Either way it wasn't very complimentary to Henry, was it, so we had words and that was the last I saw of him.'

'And that was it?'

'Yes, and it will probably stay that way. Sometimes, though, I feel out of joint with the times. There's that poem by Yeats that goes, "This is no country for old men/The young in one another's arms." I feel like that, sometimes. Everybody seems to know more about "life" than I do. Do they, Charlie? Am I missing something? Or is my condition a commonplace these days?'

'Don't ask me, Maud. I don't wander far from Annie because it's too much trouble. Not on principle, or because I don't want to. And because Annie would find out.'

'And she wouldn't like that?'

'No, she wouldn't.' Salter felt an odd sensation as if a silent vacuum had created itself on the back of his neck and he turned quickly to find yet another English middle-aged couple listening in to their conversation so hard that the man was in danger of falling off his chair. Salter turned back to Maud, who was laughing silently into her drink. 'Come on,' he said. 'Let's go back and eat.'

'You didn't really answer my question, Charlie.'

'No, and I'm not going to,' he said, pulling her to her feet and giving her a kiss for the benefit of their audience.

They found Annie and Henry in front of their hotel, drinking wine, and Salter presented Annie with the purse, happy that for once he had found a gift he was certain she would like. They all exchanged accounts of the afternoon's activities and went in search of one last, good, ten-dollar meal. After dinner the level of contentment was so high that they strolled about the town well into the small hours, reluctant to end their interlude in Florence.

'The Land of Tweedledum,' Annie said later, as they lay in bed listening to the city shutting up its doors.

Four

The Last Fence

A light drizzle was falling on Tokesbury Mallett when they arrived the next day. The change from Florence created something of a culture shock, even after so short a trip, and they had to work hard to avoid feeling depressed. The holiday was nearly over for the Beresfords, and Annie and Maud planned a last outing together. Henry, after waiting for an invitation from Salter which never came, decided to join them.

Maud watched Salter dodge any involvement with the others and asked him what he was going to do.

'I have to spend some time with the local police,' Salter said. 'The inspector there wants to show me around, and I've been putting him off.'

'And catch up with the murder?' Maud asked. 'I wonder if they've got him yet?'

'I hope so,' Annie said, looking at Salter, to whom she had promised one more day on his own to satisfy his curiosity.

'We found the brother,' Churcher said at the station the next day. 'He telephoned Boomewood and when that American girl told him what had happened he came straight back to be with his sister.'

'And?'

'Oh, he's in the clear. On the night in question he was working as a part-time helper in an Italian restaurant in Reading. Eleven Italians are prepared to testify to that and Superintendent Hamilton is inclined to believe them.' Clearly Churcher had his doubts.

'Where is he now?'

'At the hotel with his sister and the Kryst girl. They are going to reopen. The girl is going to give up the rest of her vacation to help out.'

'Now what?'

'I have no idea. I'm not in charge.'

'Any other news from Italy?'

'None, as far as I know.'

'And Dillon. Anything turned up about his past?'

'Not as far as I know. We'll find out, though. Don't worry about it.'

'I'm not. But *I* ran across something in Italy which you probably ought to know about.'

'You ran across something? In Italy?' Churcher asked unbelievingly.

'I happened to be passing through Valdottavo, the village where the card came from.'

'What card?'

Salter sighed. They really were telling Churcher nothing. He explained about the entry in the hotel register and the postcard, and then what he had learned in Valdottavo.

Churcher listened sullenly. 'So you've found out that this Dillon and Bessell were wartime chums, have you? Where does that get us?'

'It might be worth checking up on Bessell,' he said.

'I'd better report this to the superintendent,' Churcher said. 'I'll tell him you wanted to give him a message, shall I? It doesn't sound like much to me.'

If you are going to sit and sulk, thought Salter, I'm wasting my time. He made one more effort. 'Of course. But maybe you could make a couple of phone calls while you are waiting. If Bessell is alive, when he came out of the army, he must have gone somewhere, to some address. It's a long shot but just maybe he's still known there. The chances are that he went back home— he was a kid when he joined the army— and someone might remember him, even if he's moved away from the district.'

'You mean follow this up on my own?'

'You could find out his address in 1945 and let Hamilton take it from there,' Salter said. It was risky, perhaps, but he still wanted to give Churcher a boost.

'I'd better check first. It's not my investigation.' He phoned his headquarters and asked to be put through to the superintendent. Hamilton was out so Churcher left a message. 'Some information about the Dillon case has turned up,' he said, and put the phone down.

'Now what do you suggest?'

'Okay. You've covered your ass, now phone the army records office. Get the address; start the inquiry. The local station can send a man round wherever the trail starts.'

Churcher looked nervous, but slightly excited. Then, with sudden resolution, he began to make calls. Eventually he got on to someone in London with access to old army records. He listened, made notes, and after an exchange of courtesies, replaced the receiver firmly in its cradle.

'Right,' he said briskly. 'Here it is, then. Johnny Bessell was demobilized in 1945, you're quite right. His address at that time was 78 Uppingham Road, Manor Park, E.12.'

'Where's that?' Salter asked, making a casual note.

'East London. Probably quite near Ilford. I'll call the Ilford police and ask them to give us a hand.' He made another call and explained what he wanted. He listened for a while, then said, 'Yes, yes, I understand. Right, Inspector, whenever you can.'

Once more Churcher took on the look of a chastened schoolboy. 'They haven't anyone to spare at the moment,' he said. 'He's putting your request on his list and will probably call back in three or four days. It seems they have a bit of a panic going on. He asked me if I ever read the fucking papers.' Churcher reached beside his chair and took the *Daily Telegraph* out of his briefcase, and looked over the front page.

'Here it is,' he said. 'I didn't get a chance to look at it this morning. Our charlady gave in her notice and my wife was very upset.' He read out, 'Two gang leaders found dead this morning behind a public house in Manor Park.'

The sergeant put his head round the door and spoke to Churcher. 'It's Mrs Bladgett, sir. She insists on talking to you about her burglar. Would you mind? She won't be satisfied with me.'

'Of course, Sergeant,' Churcher said, looking pleased. 'I'll be right along.' To Salter he said, 'She suffers from the delusion that she is being robbed nightly, but she has a little chat with me about it and that seems to do the trick.' He walked through to the outer office.

While Salter was alone, the telephone rang and he picked it up. 'Sergeant Woodiwiss here,' a voice said. 'Superintendent Hamilton's assistant. The Superintendent is away at the moment. What's this about information on the Dillon case?'

'Inspector Churcher just left, Sergeant,' Salter said, after identifying himself. 'I'm having a cup of coffee in his office.'

'When's he coming back?'

Through the partly open door Salter could see Churcher escorting Mrs Bladgett out of the station. Sergeant Robey was busily writing at the desk. Salter took a deep breath and stepped gently out of line. 'I don't know. He left in a hurry and said goodbye to me, so it may be a while. He told me to finish my coffee.'

Woodiwiss grunted. 'Can't be very bloody important, then. Tell him to leave a message with someone here, will you?' He hung up.

Churcher returned in a few minutes, looking pleased. 'Sergeant Robey said I was wanted on the phone,' he said.

'I answered it. Just the London operator wanting to know if you'd completed your call,' Salter said, giving the lie direct which would possibly mean his neck.

'Odd. Probably British Telecom getting their lines crossed again.' He smiled. 'I think Mrs Bladgett will be all right for a couple of days. Now, what about this Dillon thing?'

'Forget about it, Charles. When you speak to Hamilton, tell him you made some phone calls at my request. A courtesy, call it, and you are reporting the request to him in case he was not aware. Tell him everything. Don't get involved. It's not your case.'

'Right, right. I think that's reasonable. Now, Charles, my wife would like to meet Mrs Salter. She wants to invite her to lunch.' Churcher beamed.

'I'll check my wife's plans,' Salter said. 'If we decide to stay much longer in the area, I'll give you a call.'

He shook hands with Churcher and waited outside the station house for the sergeant to join him.

'Nice price,' the sergeant said, looking at his boots.

'I got thirteen to two,' Salter said. He looked at his watch. 'How long will it take me to drive to London,' he asked.

'About an hour and a quarter. Take the Oxford road, then turn off on to the M40. 'Course, it depends what part.'

'Ilford.'

'Ah. Allow another hour at least, p'raps more.'

'Thanks, Sergeant.'

'No gee-gees, today, sir?' Robey inquired politely.

'No. I've got to visit some relatives of my wife.'

'Ah. Pity. When you come back then, sir.'

Salter called in at the Plough and left a

message with the host that he might be late for dinner and that Annie should go ahead without him. She and the others had gone to a sale of antiques that was taking place forty miles away.

The sergeant was right in his estimate of the time it would take him to get to London, and shortly before twelve Salter found himself in the Bayswater Road, heading for Marble Arch. He turned along Park Lane with the stream of traffic and then turned left again and stopped in a side street somewhere in Mayfair to chart the rest of his route. He was now in Curzon Street. The road was obvious: he had to work his way back to Oxford Street and then go east to something called Aldgate. But why was Oxford Street marked in white? He asked a policeman. 'Because you are not allowed in it, sir,' the constable replied, saluting. 'Your best bet is to go along Piccadilly, round the Circus, up Shaftesbury Avenue to *New* Oxford Street, and then it's a straight road all the way.'

Salter thanked him and went back to his map. It looked easy enough. He went right at the next corner, then left at Piccadilly, noticing that pedestrians had no rights in this country when a car wanted to turn a corner. He went round the Circus twice, unable to see Shaftesbury Avenue as he clung grimly to a place in the flow of traffic which surrounded him on all sides. Eventually he edged to the left and chose a likely exit and found himself in no time at all in Trafalgar Square. A friendly cab driver gave him new directions and Salter turned north. Watch out for bridges, he told himself. If I cross the Thames, I've had it. At St Giles's Circus he saw the street he wanted out of the corner of his eye and continued glumly up the Tottenham Court Road to Euston Road, which looked important, and by making three left turns got himself on to it travelling east again. When he stopped to consult his map he saw that he could make it if he stayed on this road. 'Pentonville Road, City Road, Great Eastern Street,' he chanted to himself. Then he noticed signs for the A13 which he knew was his road, and after that it was easy. When he stopped for a rest, just past Stratford where the road had turned so sharply round a church that it had unnerved him, he found that he was only three miles from his destination. It was half past one.

78 Uppingham Road was the last in a row

of small attached dwellings that looked as though they dated from the First World War. Both sides of the street were packed with cars and Salter had trouble finding somewhere to stop, jamming himself finally into a space that was technically taken up with a motor-scooter. He walked back to 78 and knocked and rang, and heard someone begin chanting immediately, 'A . . . a . . . ll ri . . . i . . . ght, a . . . a . . . ll ri . . . i . . . ght,' the sound of shuffling feet, and a dog barking furiously. The door opened six inches, and a bald, egg-shaped head appeared, wearing slightly elliptical glasses which emphasized the face's egginess. 'Yes?' he asked.

The face was only three feet from the floor, but Salter was already familiar with this phenomenon, the result of trying to speak through the door without letting the dog out, which occurs in half the houses in England. 'Wojerwant?' the face said.

Salter showed his identification. 'Can I speak to you for a moment?'

'Waffor?'

'I'm looking for a Mr Johnny Bessell. Can you help me?'

'Why?' Underneath his hand, the dog was

trying to tunnel through the floor to get at Salter.

'I'm trying to look him up. A pal of mine knew him during the war. Are you him?'

'No, I'm not. W'mminit. I'll just shut Jackie up in the scullery.'

The door closed and reopened a few minutes later and Salter was let into the tiny hallway. From the back of the house came the sounds of an enraged Jackie trying to chew his way out.

'Cuminere,' the man said. He led the way into the front room and Salter sat down in one of a pair of huge old armchairs.

'Wassertrouble?' the man asked.

'No trouble. I just want to talk to him.'

'You'll be lucky. He's been dead two years,' the little man said.

'Dead?' Salter asked, sucking air rapidly. 'Two years?'

' 'Ass right. Drowned in Lake Wossname.'

'Where?'

'Lake Toronto. In Canada.'

'There is no Lake Toronto. You mean Ontario?'

' 'Ass right.'

'You're sure?'

'I'm not sure of nothink, mate. That's

what they told me, two years ago when they came round. The police, I mean. Now, what are you up to?'

'I was just asked to look him up by a friend who knew him during the war.'

' 'Ass a load of codswallop for a start,' the man said, belligerently. 'You wouldn't show me a bleedin' mountie's card if you was just asking after a friend, would you?'

'I'm not a mountie,' Salter said. 'But you're right. I'm looking for someone else and if I had found Johnny Bessell he might have given me a lead. But you can kick me out if you want.'

'I know,' the little man said, and sniggered.

Salter stood up. He had hoped to get a few quick facts on his thin excuse, but this was getting tricky. His host was obviously a man who was proud of knowing his 'rights'. Already he could see a complaint being laid at the local police station which would earn him a roasting from Hamilton and probably Orliff, too. It was time to go.

'Don't get aereated,' the man said. 'Sit down. I'm Johnny's brother. I havn't seen him for thirty years, though. Ever since he went to Canada.'

Salter sat down again. 'What happened to him when he came out of the army?'

'He lived here for a few years, didn't he? With me. I promised Mum that I'd give him a home, didn't I? Me and the wife—she's gone, now—took over the house when Mum died before Johnny came back. He was my only family then, see, and besides, this was his home. But we never got along. The wife couldn't abide him, could she?'

'So he went to Canada?'

'After he qualified, yes. He was a Public Accountant. Got qualified and then just slung his hook. Did he get into trouble?'

'No,' said Salter patiently. 'Whereabouts did he go?'

'I dunno. Last we heard he was in this place called Toronto.'

'Did you stay in touch?'

From the scullery, the dog was howling steadily.

'No,' Bessell said. 'He wrote us cards for a few years at Christmastime, then nothing. We was never close, and after he qualified he got too good for Manor Park.'

'When was the last time you heard from him?'

'Must be twenty years ago. Must be. I was

thinking of selling the house – lot of col-
oureds were moving in – and the solicitor
told me that legally Johnny still owned half
of it, even though I'd done all the decorating
and that, because Mum had left it to both of
us. So I wrote to the last address I had and
he wrote back saying he didn't want his half.
Must have been doing all right, mustn't he?'

'And that's the last you heard of him?'

' 'Ass right. I sent him a couple of cards,
but I never heard again.'

'He never came back for a visit?'

'No, he wouldn't do that. Vera hated him.
Hated him, she did. Pity, really. She's gone
too, now, and I'm all alone, and I can't get
about much with my feet. I would have liked
to see him again. Like a cup of tea?'

'No, thanks, Mr Bessell. I'm sorry I
bothered you.'

Bessell looked at a loss. ' 'Ass all right,' he
said. 'Tell you the truth, I don't think Vera
was very nice to him. I let her drive him
away. Still, you've got to stick up for your
wife, haven't you? But it was nice of him to
give up the house, wasn't it? She couldn't
see it. Oh well. Pity I never saw him. But I
don't want to be bothered if he was in any
trouble,' he ended warningly. 'Something's

up or you wouldn't be here, would you?'

He got up to let Salter out. As the door closed behind him, Salter heard Bessell calling to his dog, assuring him that release was on the way. There was the sound of a charging animal and a thump as Jackie hurled himself against the front door. What a way to run a house, Salter thought.

He turned left at the end of the street and inserted himself into the permanent traffic jam in the Romford Road. Beside him a goggled youth waited on a throbbing motorcycle. On an impulse, Salter rolled down the window and asked the boy how he would get across London to the M40.

'Yank, eh?' the youth smiled. 'Bit of a poser, that one, mate. Friend of mine always goes on the North Circular, but I think you're best going straight through. A bit of a gamble but I've always done it. Thing is, when you get to the Bank, go along Cheapside to 'Olborn. When you get to Tottenham Court Road, go straight down Oxford Street. Bugger the signs. If they stop you, act daft.'

The lights changed and a car behind immediately began honking. The youth turned slowly on his seat. 'Shut up, you stupid git,' he snarled at the honking driver, 'or I'll come back there and sort you out.' The driver rolled up his window, and the youth turned back to Salter and smiled warmly. 'All right, guv? Don't forget: Bank, 'Olborn, Oxford Street. Got it?' The lights changed to yellow and he and Salter ducked through, leaving the car behind to wait for another change.

Tweedledum *and* Tweedledee, thought Salter.

In Tokesbury Mallet that evening, Salter explained to Annie what was going on.

'Bessell drowned two years ago in Lake Ontario,' he concluded.

'But that girl in Valdottavo said that Dillon told her that he died in Italy when they were trying to escape!'

'Right. Why? What happened in those hills?'

'Dillon might just have *assumed* he was dead. If he was listed as missing and Dillon never checked after the war, I mean.'

'They were buddies. He would have gone to see Bessell's family.'

'How could he? He went missing himself.

He wouldn't have wanted to take any chances.'

Salter thought about this. 'Maybe,' he said. 'Maybe. But nothing else is explained, is it?'

'You mean the Rundstedt woman?'

'And Parrott. The guy who took me racing. He lived in Toronto for a while. There are too many connections to Toronto.'

'Dillon?'

'Maybe.'

'You think that Rundstedt and Dillon and Bessell and Parrott are all connected? It sounds a little wild, Charlie.'

'That's what Orliff would say. But it's a lot of coincidences, isn't it?'

'So are we.'

'What?'

'So are *we*. We're Canadian, from Toronto. On that basis Hamilton should have checked up on us right away.'

'Oh, he did.'

'*What?*'

'Listen, love. When you find a body in a hotel with half a dozen handy suspects you check up on all of them.'

'Me too?'

'Sure!'

'What's your guess, then? About this whole gang?'

'Something like this. Dillon and his wartime buddy knew about each other, maybe they met in Toronto, but for some reason, when Dillon visited Valdottavo he made up a story about Bessell having died in Tuscany. Maybe he knew that Bessell was now really dead. I'm sure that Rundstedt knew Dillon, and I'm guessing that Parrott and Rundstedt were more than just bedmates in the Swan for a night. I think they may have had something on Dillon, something to do with Bessell.'

'So what are you going to do about it?'

'Tell Hamilton in the morning. I think Hamilton has written off the postcard, and he's still trying to track down someone who had a grudge against Dillon.' Salter smiled. 'Combing the underworld, probably. It'll be fun telling him about Bessell.'

'Tomorrow morning, then? Then back to our holiday?'

'Of course.'

'I think you're playing with fire, Charlie. Hamilton's not going to be pleased, is he?'

'Probably not. That's the idea.'

'Okay. But I would like to be driving

north the day after tomorrow.'

'You will be,' Salter said.

'Good. Because the forecast is for some cloudiness in the north-west. It might be breaking up. Anyway, I'm losing my chum. Maud and Henry are going home.'

'Tomorrow?'

'Yes. Maud paid us the nicest compliment this afternoon, by the way, while we were in Coutsbury. She said it has been the best holiday she has had since she and Henry got married.'

'She did? All because of us?'

'Mostly. She told me that before the holiday she and Henry had been having problems.'

'Why? Henry seems all right. And they seemed a good couple – she wants to know everything about everybody and Henry doesn't give a damn for anything except rats. What was the problem? Henry got a girl-friend? Or Maud a boyfriend?'

'Nothing like that. Just the opposite. Henry, apparently, can't get enough of her, and she still likes him, loves him, I think. That surprise you?'

'Nothing surprises me about other people's lives except the fact that they talk about them. But she couldn't stand him? In bed, I mean?'

'Not that, either. She just felt she was leading a very narrow life, and she is smart enough to believe that her curiosity about everybody is a bit old-maidish. Some stupid pal of Henry's told her this. He said she was substituting curiosity for experience, and it was an appetite that would grow, he said, by what it fed on. He suggested that she should fulfil herself, experience life, instead of living through other people. She even wondered if she and Henry should separate.'

'So what happened?' Salter asked. He had not told Annie about his conversation with Maud in Florence.

'That's where we came in. She talked to me a lot — there's nothing like someone you will never see again for having a good heart-to-heart. That's why she wanted to stay with us even to going to Florence. She saw us — *us*, Charlie — as people of the world and she pumped me — no, that's not fair — *asked* me to tell her just what was going on with our generation, theirs and ours, today.'

'You didn't tell her, I hope.'

'Sure, I did. She's certainly incredibly naive in her assumptions about other people's lives. Unless I am. No, she is. She put it well; she's always been a great reader and playgoer and when she was young the books and plays reflected life as she knew it. But lately, in the last ten years, nothing seems like anything she knows about. She began to feel as if she were like the Lady of Shallott. Life passing her by.'

'And now she doesn't. Just from talking to you?'

'I think she's taken comfort from living with us, Charlie. At any rate she's going back to Watford happy, feeling she's very lucky to have Henry, and looking forward to an interesting old age.'

'But a lot less nosey, eh?'

'I guess so. She says that she realized that under the tranquil surface of most people's lives lies a stagnant pond.'

Just from talking to me? Salter wondered.

'What about Henry? Is he aware of all this?' he asked.

'We didn't talk much about him, but he has his own anxieties, I think. He made a pass at me in Florence.'

'For Christ's sake!'

'Nothing serious. He put his arm around me in the Piazza del Duomo. I think he was just being gallant, in case that's what Canadians did.'

'The bastard,' Salter said. He laughed. 'Well, well, well, I'll challenge him to a duel, shall I?'

'You won't say a word. Now go and put a tie on for dinner. They'll be down soon.'

But before he went up to their room, Salter put a call in to Toronto, and spoke to his sergeant. The call was returned before he had finished dressing.

'What did you find out, Frank?' he asked. He was tying his tie with one hand, standing up at the front desk because the Plough did not run to telephones in the guests' bedrooms. Annie watched him from the bar.

Gatenby, Salter's cosy-voiced, white-haired assistant, began. 'I'll read you everything I've got,' he said. 'First. John Stanley Bessell is a missing person.' There was a long pause. 'That's helpful, isn't it, Charlie?'

'Read the bloody thing right through, Frank. We'll chat about it when I get home, not at ten dollars a minute.'

'Sorry. Well then, Johnny Bessell is, or was a missing person. He went sailing in Lake Ontario two years ago. His sailboat was found empty off Scarborough Bluffs but he never turned up. He's officially dead now. There was no sign he left the country and he's never turned up anywhere else. It was listed as accidental with a possibility of suicide, because he was a good sailor.'

'Why would he have committed suicide?'

'He was going to be in trouble with us. The Fraud Squad, that is. He was a partner in a small construction company with a fella named Cossitt, Michael Cossitt, and when we investigated the incident a few things turned up, then a lot more. You want me to read all this, Charlie? It's about twenty pages of summation of what they were up to.'

'What sort of things?'

'Skimming. Income tax evasion. Fraud. There were thirty-seven charges finally.'

'What happened?'

'Cossitt, the partner, went to jail. He denied everything. Said Bessell was entirely responsible for the books and he knew nothing about it. But his name was on the cheques, and he had more money than he should have according to the income tax declaration, so they got him on that.'

'And Bessell never turned up?'

'No. Why?'

'I'm curious. This guy came back to life

once already. What about Dillon?'

'Nothing on him. He never immigrated here officially. The Immigration Department know nothing about him, nor does anyone else.'

'Shit. And Rundstedt?'

'We've already had an inquiry about her. From the bobbies over there. Nothing at all. She's just a nice Canadian lady on holiday.'

'Parrott?'

'Another blank. Nobody here has heard of him.'

'Okay. Thanks. I'll get back to you if I want anything else.' Salter rang off and joined Annie in the bar.

'Got an idea, Charlie?' she asked.

'I just thought I'd check them all out with Frank before I hand it over to Hamilton. I wish I hadn't now. Bessell *was* drowned in Lake Ontario. Rundstedt *is* what she seems to be, and they've never heard of Dillon or Parrott.'

'So much for the great Canadian conspiracy.'

'I guess so. But I dunno. There's still something screwy. Parrott told me he had worked for the Manitoba Government, and he knew about stuff like Greenwood racetrack. But Gatenby says there's no record of him anywhere.' He shrugged. 'I've run out of things to do, that's for sure.'

'Good,' Annie said. 'Here come Maud and Henry now.'

'You're leaving, I hear,' Salter said to Henry when they were seated in the dining-room.

'On our way tomorrow,' Henry said. 'It's been very nice knowing you, Charlie. You've saved us from a fate worse than death— three weeks in an English hotel in the pouring rain. What about you?'

'Oh yes. We enjoyed ourselves.'

'No, I meant, are you staying here much longer?'

'We are leaving almost immediately for the Lake District,' Annie said.

'In a day or so, anyway,' Salter said.

A bottle of unordered wine appeared on their table. 'What's this?' Henry asked.

'Found it in the stores,' their landlord said, over his shoulder, or rather, to the kitchen doorway. 'Not on inventory. Surplus to requirements. On the house.'

'How nice,' said Maud, who was the first to recover. 'We'll come back here.'

'That's the idea,' the host said to the notice-board.

The next morning Salter asked Churcher for half an hour to talk about an idea he had had. During the night he had worked out a theory which made sense of Gatenby's information, or lack of it.

'I see. I see,' Churcher said. 'So you think this man Bessell, who died in Italy, then again in Canada, is still alive?'

'I think he *may* be. If it sounds dumb to you, don't pass it on.'

'It sounds like a bit of a fairy tale to me. Now, the second point. You also think he was in the village on the night of the murder. Calling himself Parrott?'

'I think Parrott *may* be Bessell, yes.'

'And you think Bessell somehow got hold of something sleazy in Dillon's past and was blackmailing him?'

'Or the opposite. That Dillon knew something about Bessell's disappearance and was blackmailing *him*.'

Salter watched Churcher trying to hold both possibilities in his head at once.

'The first is more likely, isn't it?' Churcher said. 'There's the card from

224

Valdottavo, the entry in the hotel register—both of them suggest that Bessell approached Dillon. And Dillon, after all, was a deserter and might have been doing anything for the last thirty years.'

Salter conceded the point. 'These two guys were together in Italy,' he resumed. 'They got separated. Only one of them returned, apparently, but the other one finally turned up. Whatever was going on probably dated from then. One of them—Dillon, say—let the other one down, and so long as the other guy was dead anyway, that was the end of it. Bessell survived, forgot about his pal, but maybe ran across him—' Salter stopped. 'Of course,' he said. 'Dillon went back to Valdottavo two years ago and met his wife in Lucca. A sentimental journey. If Bessell had the same idea, a coincidence, but possible, he would have found out about Dillon, learned about his English address and come after him. There was a guy asking after Dillon in Valdottavo a month ago. Bessell. But why wasn't he showing himself?'

Churcher looked cunning. 'Because it wasn't a coincidence, Charles. Somehow he must have found out that this Dillon who had let him down was still alive and started to look for him in Valdottavo where he knew he might have visited.'

'Good. Let's not fuck around any more, Charles. Have you found out any more about Dillon?'

'Not much. He was an orphan, apparently. Went into the army as a boy in the Thirties. He might have met up with Bessell in North Africa, before the Italian front opened.'

'Why was he still a private?'

'He went up and down to corporal and back twice, but he was often in trouble. A bit of a maverick, apparently. Commended for resourcefulness several times, twice punished for being absent without leave and lost his stripes both times.'

'In fact just the sort of guy to finagle his way back to England and disappear into the streets rather than go back to the front. Only Bessell knew what really happened up there in Tuscany, and Dillon knew that Bessell wouldn't or couldn't testify that he was still alive.'

'He certainly sounds like a wide boy.'

'A what?'

'What we call his type. It means artful, on the fiddle, sticky-fingered. A kind of Duddy Kravitz.' Churcher looked proudly at Salter, waiting for him to catch the reference.

'I thought the only Canadian the English had ever heard of was Honest Ed,' Salter said, in acknowledgement of Churcher's learning.

'My wife reads a lot,' Churcher said. 'She recommends things to me. I have very little time for reading myself, but I do try and read one new book a month.'

'All right. You haven't found out anything about Dillon after the war?'

'Not as far as I know.'

'And the others, Parrott and Rundstedt — are they known to you?'

'I don't think so.' Churcher looked uncomfortable.

'I'm getting convinced that Parrott *is* Bessell, Charles. He *has* to be.'

'But it's just a wild guess, isn't it?'

'Not so wild. I know that he was pumping people about me. I am pretty sure either he or Dillon went through my clothes and found out I was a copper. It makes sense to me that Parrott and Dillon knew each other. It also makes sense that our Miss Rundstedt is involved. Parrott was her alibi, if she needed one, but no one bothered to notice that she was Parrott's alibi, too. Hamilton wasn't looking at Parrott. Do you know how far Hamilton checked him out?'

'We took a statement from him, of course, just to eliminate Rundstedt. As you know she was — what was your phrase? — shacked up with him on the night Dillon was killed. She has it off with anybody, it seems. A woman like that causes nothing but trouble, don't you think? I mean, according to Mario and Mrs Dillon, Dillon had never so much as looked at another woman since his marriage — certainly not at any of the guests — until she turned up, wiggling her rump at him. Bloody tart.'

'Bloody *Canadian* tart, you mean.' Salter wondered if he should give up on this man. Hadn't he been listening to anything? One more try. 'What I am suggesting, Charles, is that just maybe she wasn't screwing Dillon. She may have been in cahoots with Parrott. Some kind of go-between, known to both Parrott and Dillon. The conversation the Smarmy Boy overheard sounded to me like a long talk about something more serious than screwing.'

'Perhaps. I think I'd better call Superintendent Hamilton now and let him know what you think. I gave him your message about what you'd found out about Bessell.'

So that little trick didn't work. I might as well have told Woodiwiss myself. 'What did he say?' Salter asked.

'He called you a clever-dick and hung up.' Churcher blushed, but he looked slightly pleased, too.

'I'll tell you what,' Salter offered. 'Call him and tell him I just dropped by to let you know I'd like to talk to him. And that I'll call him myself this afternoon.'

'All right. That makes sense. It's not my case anyway, is it?'

'Good. Now come and have a beer and a sandwich with me.' Salter was eager to keep Churcher away from the telephone.

'I usually eat a sandwich at my desk, Charles, to save time. The wife puts one in my briefcase.' He hauled out a paper-wrapped sandwich and held it up.

The war against crime in Tokesbury Mallett waged ceaselessly on, Salter thought, while the soldiers ate at their posts. 'Eat it tomorrow,' he said. 'This is on me.'

'Good-oh, then. The Swan?'

'No, not the Swan. The Eagle and Child.'

'The old Bird and Baby, eh. Right you are, Charles.'

Salter was glad to see some jauntiness creeping back into Churcher's manner. He would probably survive.

'I think after all I'd better let Superintendent Hamilton know about this idea of yours, Charles, in case there's anything in it,' Churcher said as soon as they were back in the office.

'I guess so. Cover your ass. Things might warm up. Let's just say I walked in and sprang this on you, shall we? Call Hamilton and relay my message.'

Churcher dialled Hamilton and told him what Salter had said. Then he listened for a few moments and put the phone down, looking frightened. 'He wants us both at headquarters immediately,' he said. 'He sounds in a bit of a temper.'

He can't do anything to me, thought Salter.

'Been doing a bit of sleuthing, have you, Salter?' Hamilton asked as soon as they walked into his office. 'Hands across the sea, is it? All right, tell me again what you have deduced. Leave us alone, will you, Churcher? I'm about to give this man the

230

bollocking of his life. You shouldn't have to watch it.'

The door closed behind Churcher, and Hamilton nodded for Salter to tell his tale. Once again Salter reminded himself that Hamilton could only complain as far as he was concerned, and he told the story of how, while he was in Italy, he had picked up a thread that wound through Toronto back to Tokesbury Mallett.

'So what do we conclude then, *Inspector?*' Hamilton's manner was jeering, but he did not seem very angry.

'I think it's a reasonable surmise that Johnny Bessell came over here when he disappeared from Toronto, maybe with some of the money he's accused of taking. He found out that Dillon, his old wartime chum, was still alive, had something on him and started blackmailing him. He went too far and Dillon pulled a knife. There was a fight and Dillon got killed. So Bessell took off.'

'Where to?'

Salter shrugged. 'You'll find him. Get a description from Toronto.' Screw you, Bulstrode.

'Good, goo-ood,' Hamilton said. 'So now we know he's a compatriot of yours. But

231

otherwise we are back where we came in, looking for the mysterious entry in the hotel register who we *think* is Johnny Bessell?' Hamilton paused, and added. 'A man there is no record of having passed through Tuscany in the past three months, according to the *polizia*.'

Salter shrugged. So the English are more awake than I thought. If you hadn't played your cards so close to your chest we wouldn't be sitting here now, waltzing round your office, he thought, forgetting for the moment that he had no right to know anything. 'You checked the Valdottavo end?' he asked.

'Of course we bloody checked the sodding Valdottavo end. Not, I may say, by poncing about with the local peasants, but by calling our friends in Lucca who dug out the Dillon/Bessell story in a couple of hours. We've been looking for him ever since.'

'When I was in Valdottavo, the locals said nothing about anyone else having inquired,' Salter said, his curiosity overcoming the desire to avoid humiliation.

Hamilton laughed with the sound of a paper bag bursting. 'You should have asked the *polizia* in Lucca. They asked the *carabinieri* in Valdottavo for us. The story's well-known. Mind you, the *polizia* wouldn't have told you anything. They were requested not to talk to Canadian coppers.'

'You knew I was going to Valdottavo?' Salter asked.

'Why else would you suddenly fly orf to Pisa? Not to see the sodding leaning tower. Perhaps just because it was raining in Tokesbury Mallett and it seemed like a good idea at the time?' Hamilton laughed again. He was having a wonderful time.

'Sergeant Woodiwiss,' Salter said, after a few moments. 'He saw me coming out of the travel agency. You've been keeping tabs on me.'

'You raised his curiosity, Salter. And mine. I wondered how far you'd go. And now you've caught up. We'd have heard what you were up to without Woodiwiss, by the way. One of the locals thought you were very suspicious— don't ever retire and go into business for yourself, Salter— and they told the *carabinieri* who phoned me yesterday, to tell me you'd been tiptoeing through the Tuscan hills. So we are back where we started, looking for the mysterious Johnny. Got any suggestions?'

'Not at the moment,' Salter said, feeling a keen sense of kinship with Churcher.

'If you do get any more ideas, let me know, will you? I might be able to save you some trouble. As you know, Johnny Bessell has not been seen around Manor Park lately.'

Salter stared at him. 'When I talked to his brother, he didn't say he had already been questioned by the cops. You people.'

He regretted it immediately. Hamilton bared his teeth. 'He hadn't, then. But when we heard that you had gone to see him, the Ilford boys popped round afterwards to see what you were up to. Thanks for the tip. We knew about Bessell's old home address, of course, but in view of other information in our hands we didn't think there was any point. Until you decided to have a chat with the brother yourself.'

'I didn't tell anyone where I was going,' Salter said.

Hamilton watched him until Salter found the answer to his own question. 'Sergeant Robey?' Salter asked.

'Well done, Salter, well done. Yes, yes. Robey heard you lying your head orf to Sergeant Woodiwiss on Churcher's phone, and he called Woodiwiss back after you left for London. The fact is, old boy, we've been watching you stumble across our screen from the beginning. You haven't done too badly.'

'Thank you,' Salter said. 'You still haven't got Bessell, have you?'

'We will. We will. And now I suggest that you lay orf. All right? We can manage on our own.'

Salter stood up, feeling slightly foolish. A thought, nearly impossible, struck him. 'Churcher,' he said. 'Is he in on your game?'

'No, Salter, he is not, as you say, in on my game, nor is he on yours, I gather. Let's leave him out, shall we? He's got his own problems.'

On that note Salter allowed Churcher to drive him back to the Plough in near silence. There he persuaded the landlady to make him a pot of tea which he took into the residents' lounge, hoping to be left alone.

Hamilton had left him feeling raw, and he had a strong need to score at least a couple of points before the Englishman found Parrott and wrapped it up, or not. Salter ruminated about the actors, or what he was assuming were the actors in the case. Parrott was Bessell and Parrott/Bessell was leaning on

Dillon, he was guessing. So what was Rundstedt's role? An observation of Maud's came to mind and he wondered how far Hamilton had checked her out. One last call.

He finished his tea and phoned Gatenby, his assistant in Toronto.

'Frank, I want you to check up on Rundstedt, for me. I know, I know. You already did. She's just a nice lady on holiday. Now push it a bit harder. She may have changed her name in the last two or three years. So try everything you can think of. The passport office, maybe. But find out who she was and everything about her. Call me here when you know something. Tell Orliff what you are doing. Tell him the honour of the Force is at stake.'

The act of asking the question provided the answer and by the time Gatenby phoned back, after dinner, Salter had already guessed.

'Bingo, Charlie,' Gatenby said. 'I found her in the morgue at the *Globe and Mail*. Miss Rundstedt is the former Mrs Bessell. After her husband disappeared she changed back to her single name, to avoid people, I suppose. She appeared at the trial, too, I think. And she went back to work.'

'You didn't tell the English coppers any of this?'

'We didn't know it, did we? I just found all this out.'

'Good. That's it for now, Frank.'

'Oh, Charlie. I told Mr Orliff what you were up to and he said to warn you that Hamilton has probably got you on a bit of string in a glass tank. What does that mean, Charlie?'

'I'm finding out, Frank. But we'll see.' He hung up and dialled the Swan identifying himself as Churcher's assistant. 'Miss Rundstedt?' he asked.

'She left three days ago. I told the inspector already.'

'I know. I just want to get her forwarding address again.'

'Only her Canadian one. Would you like that?'

'No, thanks. All right.'

He had no resources which would help him find Rundstedt, and it was time for him to let Hamilton know about this latest call. First thing in the morning, he promised himself.

He went back to the bar and told Annie the story, or as much of it as she didn't already know.

'OK, Charlie,' she said. 'Phone Hamilton in the morning and let's get going.'

But he had one last problem. 'Mrs Churcher is calling on you in the morning,' he said. 'She wants to invite you to lunch before you go.'

'Oh, for God's sake. Was this your idea?'

'It's either that or dinner. I've put Churcher off three times now. We have a choice.'

'All right. And tomorrow night I want to go to the best restaurant in Stratford and I want front row seats for the play.'

'You're on,' Salter said. She was letting him off lightly, he thought, as he went in search of his host for advice on restaurants.

Before breakfast the next morning he put in a call to Hamilton who was not yet in the office, and left a message to be contacted at the Plough. The call was returned in half an hour.

'I'm in Tokesbury Mallett,' Hamilton said. 'What do you want.'

Salter considered. 'I'll come and talk to you there,' he said. He poked his head into the dining-room. 'I'll be an hour, dear,' he said, and ran off before she could reply.

'Still on the trail, Salter?' Hamilton jeered. 'Always get your man, do you?'

'That's the mounties, sir. They do it on horseback. I just wanted to tell you something I learned about the Rundstedt woman.'

'How did you learn it, Salter, and when? Don't give up easily, do you? I thought I'd told you to fuck orf.'

'I was talking to my sergeant last night about some other problems, and we got chatting about this case. He's been handling your inquiries, you see, and my name has cropped up.'

'Yes. I told Orliff you were buggering about.'

Bloody liar. The first thing you did was check up on a potentially bent copper with a taste for homicide. 'Anyway,' Salter said. 'He remembered something about Rundstedt after you called. Got a memory like an elephant, Gatenby has. It seems she recently changed her name.'

'Oh, really. What was her old name — Toronto Rose?'

'Mrs Bessell.'

Hamilton stuck a finger in his ear and

rotated the side of his face while he considered this. 'Mrs Johnny Bessell?'

'Yes. The wife, or widow, of our missing person.'

'So they were operating together? A shakedown team?' Hamilton rotated the side of his head again. 'So Bessell faked his suicide to dodge the music? Later he ran across Dillon, probably picked up the trail in Italy, and together with his wife tried to get some money off him? It would explain why Dillon was in her room, and all the chat that wanker overheard. I've been trying to fit that in.'

'So have I. It fits now.'

'This means Bessell and his wife have been hand in glove all along? From the fake suicide right up to now? Somehow they have stayed in touch?'

'Maybe. They've been in touch lately, anyway, and now Bessell's wartime buddy is dead and some money was to change hands. She's involved, all right.'

'Isn't she, though? We shall have to have words with her.'

'You could trace her through the car rental company, like the American girl. It shouldn't take a couple of days.'

'It'll take an hour. She left here three days ago when her boyfriend left. Not with him, though. She is now in a hotel in Clodbury, about forty miles away. You don't think we waved her bye-bye, do you?' Hamilton smiled and went back to a piece of paper he was scribbling on. 'Let me finish this and we'll be off. If you want to come with me.'

All right, thought Salter. You win. You didn't know she was Mrs Bessell, though, did you?

While he waited for Hamilton, he pondered the possibility that Rundstedt herself was the killer. But she had an alibi, and even apart from the word of Parrott, now much in doubt, the hotel employees had confirmed that she had spent the night with him and been seen about the hotel at roughly the time of the death. Salter had another thought.

'Before we go, let's call in at the Swan,' he said.

'Why?'

'And bring that postcard from Valdottavo with you.'

'Why?'

'I'll tell you on the way. Ready?'

'Righto. Have your fun. The Swan it is.'

At the hotel Salter asked to see the register, and turned back to the entries of a week before.

'You won't find Bessell there, you silly sod,' Hamilton said. 'Churcher may not be bright, but he is efficient. He checked all these hotels when I took the case over.'

Salter ignored him. 'There,' he said. He put the message on the postcard underneath Parrott's name in the hotel register.

'Ah,' Hamilton said. 'It's the same writing all right. Don't lose this register,' he barked at the clerk. 'Put it in the safe. On second thoughts — ' he reached over and tore the page out. 'You want a receipt?'

The clerk recovered himself. 'Only for police purposes,' he said.

'I *am* the police, laddie,' Hamilton snarled.

'So I gathered,' the clerk said, pointing to the mangled register. 'Who else?'

In the car on the way to Clodbury, Hamilton mused. 'So Rundstedt and your pal Parrott are Bessell and Bessell. Blackmailing Dillon? Right?'

'It's not that certain yet. She might have been looking for Bessell herself. She probably knew the Bessell/Dillon story. Maybe she had a grudge against her husband,

242

somehow turned up Dillon, and Dillon told her Bessell had appeared. Or better yet, when Bessell found Dillon, Dillon might have contacted Rundstedt.'

'If, if, if. Why would Dillon make contact with a woman he'd never met? Just to see if she had a grudge against her husband?'

'I don't know, do I? I'm just trying to adapt. This is an English murder. Where I come from we don't get too many of these clever cases. We deal mostly with mad trappers. But maybe Dillon did know her. In Canada. We don't know where he spent the last thirty years.'

'All right now, Salter. Shut up for a minute and let me think.'

A few minutes later, Hamilton pulled up in front of the Clodbury Arms and pointed across the street. 'That's our man, there,' he said contemptuously. A boy in a blond beard and sandals was standing outside a betting shop, reading the *Sporting Life*.

They walked over to him.

'Very clever, Simpson,' Hamilton said. 'Next time you go to the races, though, have a look and see how many of the punters are wearing open-toed sandals. You look like a Jesus freak. Where is she?'

'In the teashop, sir. She went in about twenty minutes ago. Should have finished by now.'

'Right. You know her by sight, Salter? Good. Okay, laddie. We'll take over now. Go and have your morning carrot juice and report back to Sergeant Woodiwiss.'

Five minutes later Rundstedt appeared in the doorway of the teashop, checked the sky for signs of rain and walked down the High Street to the Clodbury Arms. They waited until she was well inside, then followed her in. Hamilton identified himself. 'A little chat, Miss Rundstedt,' he said and steered her into the unopened bar. Salter had a word with the alarmed landlord, and shut the door.

'Now, Miss Rundstedt. Where shall we begin? At the end, I think. Where is Johnny Bessell?'

Rundstedt reacted satisfactorily. Her eyes widened, her face went white, and she started to walk backwards.

'Sit down,' Hamilton ordered. 'You too, Salter. So the name is familiar, is it? Johnny Bessell, your husband. Now, where is he?'

Rundstedt looked from one to the other without saying anything.

'You are Mrs Bessell?' Hamilton pressed her.

She nodded, jerking her head once.

'So where is husband Johnny?'

'He's dead. He drowned in Lake Ontario, two years ago.'

'No, he isn't. He's around here somewhere, calling himself Jeremy Parrott. That right, Salter? Now where?' Hamilton had become terrifying, a schoolmaster in a child's nightmare.

Rundstedt began to tremble, and Hamilton shook her hard. 'Landlord,' he bawled. 'Make some tea. Strong and sweet.'

The cure for everything, thought Salter irrelevantly.

Rundstedt's teeth began to chatter, and Hamilton shook her again. Slowly she recovered herself and when the tea came she drank it greedily.

'Now,' Hamilton resumed.

'I don't know,' she said. 'I don't know where he is.'

'But he's not dead, is he?'

She shook her head and stared at Hamilton. 'No,' she said in a little girl voice.

'Then where is he?'

'I don't have any arrangement with him, I

told you. I don't want to see him. I just want him to leave me alone.'

Hamilton sat back in his chair. 'All right, Mrs Bessell. Mind if I call you that? Yes, I know you are Rundstedt now, legally, but my calling you Mrs Bessell means I can think more clearly about what you are up to. All right? Good. Mrs Bessell, tell us, would you, about the amazing series of coincidences that have brought you, your suicidal husband, and his once-dead army mate all to Tokesbury Mallett at the same time. And how, by chance, one of you got killed.'

'I don't know anything about that. Nor does Johnny. He was with me when it happened.'

'So you say. And all the hotel staff confirm that you spent the night in his room when Dillon was killed. Reliving old days, Mrs Bessell?'

Rundstedt was white-faced and beginning to tremble again. 'It's got nothing to do with you, has it?' she said. Then she found some defiance. 'I screw everybody. Haven't you heard?'

Hamilton reversed himself immediately and became avuncular. 'I'm sorry if I offended you,' he said. 'But I do want to

246

know how you and Bessell and Dillon got here. And I don't think you do screw everybody. Nor do I care. Now tell me your story. What are you doing here? Eh?'

To Salter, Hamilton now looked like Wackford Squeers putting on a show for the parents of a new boy, but it seemed to work.

'Someone told me they'd seen Johnny,' she said. 'So I came over.' She was beginning to recover now, her defiance had given her some energy, and she collected herself in her chair and crossed her legs.

'Who?' Hamilton said coaxingly.

She shrugged. 'I don't know. I got a postcard from here. All it said was: "Johnny Bessell is alive and well and living in Tokesbury Mallett." '

'That sounds like a joke. Why did you take it seriously?'

'Because I never thought he was dead,' Rundstedt said immediately. 'I always knew he'd turn up. So I took my holidays and came over here.'

'And he was here? Where did you find him?'

'In the pub. On the first day.'

'And? Go on?'

'He told me he had found Dillon, his army

buddy, and he had something on him.'

'What? What did he have on him?'

'I don't know. He said he'd been tracking him down for a long time and now he knew what Dillon had been doing when he was supposed to be dead, and Dillon was going to pay for deserting him during the war.'

'He was going to blackmail him?'

'So he said. And he tried to get me to go along with it.'

'Tried? You didn't go along?'

'No, I didn't. Bloody Johnny Bessell has ruined my life and I wasn't going to play his game. So I just pretended to, that's all.'

'What *did* you do?'

Now that Rundstedt was properly launched, Hamilton stopped his ingratiating pose and returned to the headmaster's role.

'I double-crossed him. I told Dillon everything.'

'While you pretended to go along with your husband?'

'Yes. My idea was that Dillon could pretend to be scared, then he could just as easily blackmail Johnny, who was still wanted by the Toronto police, something he thought Dillon wouldn't know.'

'And what would you get out of it?'

'Nothing. I just wanted to stop Johnny's little game. I planned to leave when Johnny realized that it was no go.'

'You're lying, Mrs Bessell, aren't you? You planned to have Bessell blackmail Dillon, then you would get the money as your price for not exposing Bessell. A dangerous game.'

Rundstedt looked confused at this. Then her eyes widened and she shrugged. 'Suit yourself,' she said. 'I don't want any part of it now, I'll tell you that, Mister.'

'So what went wrong?'

'I don't know. Dillon got killed, didn't he? By that waiter.'

'Now you're lying again, aren't you? Bessell killed Dillon and made you give him an alibi. You knew that, didn't you? Bessell killed Dillon.'

'No, he didn't. He was with me all night. But I got scared so I ran away and came here to wait for my plane. I'm on a charter flight and it doesn't leave until Sunday, so I came here to use up the rest of my holiday.'

'Bessell killed Dillon. You know that. Now, where is Bessell?'

Rundstedt burst into tears, but this time there was no hysteria behind them. 'I don't know,' she wailed. 'I didn't want any more to do with it. I told him to leave me alone.'

Hamilton went over the ground several times, but she would not be budged. All she wanted was to be left alone, she said.

'All right, Mrs Bessell,' Hamilton said suddenly. 'We'll find him. Before you leave, probably, and then we'll see, shall we? Enjoy your holiday.' He stood up and nodded to Salter.

Just like that? thought Salter. Then he remembered Hamilton's favourite technique of leaving people on a leash. He probably has my wife staked out, he thought.

The two policemen moved into the street and Hamilton led the way around the block to a truck which was parked behind the hotel. He opened the back door and motioned Salter in ahead of him. Inside, a young man in overalls sat listening to headphones. Hamilton nodded to him and sat down on a bench on one side, making room for Salter to sit beside him.

'Now,' Hamilton said. 'When was she lying?'

'She was covering for Bessell,' Salter offered. 'She ran away because she knew

Bessell had killed Dillon.'

'Right. And the rest of it? This double blackmail rubbish?'

'Two things bother me. Why was Bessell blackmailing Dillon if they were such pals during the war?' He told Hamilton of the friendship between Dillon and Bessell he had learned about in Italy. 'And how did Bessell get her to cooperate with him in the first place.'

'We don't know what went on at the end in Tuscany in 1944, do we? Rundstedt says Dillon betrayed Bessell. We'll have to wait and see. As for the second, Bessell apparently persuaded her that there was money to be made out of Dillon. That was before she saw that she could make some money *and* get her revenge.' As he spoke each name Hamilton paused as if he had to constantly remind himself who he was talking about.

Salter remained doubtful. They were interrupted by the technician. 'Here she is, now sir,' he said. He flicked a switch and they heard the telephone voice of Rundstedt asking to speak to Arnold Burton. A male voice responded, 'Burton here.'

'They've been here,' Mrs Bessell said immediately. 'I told them the story, but I don't think they believed me. About knowing where you are I mean. They are going to come back, I know it.'

'All right, calm down. Did you stick to the story? Every word?'

'Yes, I did. But they know you did it. If they come back, I'll make a slip, I know I will. I'm scared. I don't want any more to do with it. I'm going away. How did they know where I was?'

'I told you. They're looking for me. That whole village is crawling with coppers. All you have to do is shut up and keep telling them what I told you. They won't find me if you do what I told you. They don't even know who they are looking for. So don't worry.'

'I can't keep it up. If they come back I'll give in, I know I will. I'm going.'

There was a long pause. Then, 'You want me to meet you?'

'Yes, I do. Tell me what to do next. One of those policemen is really terrible. I'm an accessory now. It's not fair. All I wanted was to get my own back.'

'Where are you now?'

'In the hotel.'

'Fucking *hell*. Okay. Meet me by the fence

252

like I told you. Don't say anything more on the phone.'

'When?'

'Leave now. They'll probably follow you, but don't panic. Do it like I told you.' He hung up.

'Well, well, well,' Hamilton said when they were in the street again. 'I thought *some* of it was true, didn't you? Never mind. She shall have bells on her wherever she goes. He was right about that. We'll catch him, sooner or later. I wonder where that fence is? The names are interesting— Bessell, Parrott, Burton, I suppose he changes names every time he moves. That *was* Parrott, I suppose? Your racing pal? The thing is, unless we get him now we might never get him. He's right; we don't know who we're looking for and it would be a hell of a job to track him down.'

'What are you talking about? You're looking for a guy named Johnny Bessell. You've got a description. Christ, you can get a photograph and fingerprints from Toronto. You might have to wait until he turns up at an airport, but you'll get him eventually.'

Hamilton, for the first time in Salter's experience, looked confused. If the idea were not absurd, he might have thought Hamilton was blushing.

'Right, right, right, right,' Hamilton said. 'Right, right. I'm despairing too soon. We'll get him. Let's set the wheels in motion.' He led Salter out of the truck to a car opposite the hotel parking lot where two young men were waiting. He leaned into the driver's window to give him instructions. The driver nodded, and Hamilton took Salter off for a stroll down the high street. 'Let's wait a few minutes, shall we? he said. 'See if we get instant action.'

Almost immediately Rundstedt came out of the hotel and got into a car parked in the hotel lot. She drove off followed by the police car Hamilton had briefed.

'We'll follow in a few minutes. No rush. Once my men get Bessell in their sights they know what to do. Let's have a drink, shall we?' He pointed to the Clodbury Arms, and the two men walked into the bar where Hamilton ordered beer.

'You seem quiet, Salter,' Hamilton said. 'Thinking clever thoughts, are we?'

Hamilton's moment of embarrassment had exploded a tiny bomb in Salter's brain. Half way through the beer he saw how it had all been done. 'I was thinking I had better phone my wife,' he said. 'Do I have time?'

'Certainly. I think we can give them another ten minutes. There's a phone-box in the lobby.'

'The one you've got bugged?' Salter asked.

Hamilton laughed. 'I've sent that lad home,' he said. 'I have to watch every penny.'

It took Salter very little time to get through to Gatenby in Toronto, who gave him again the story of Bessell's suicide, as well as a full description of the man they were following. Then he phoned Tokesbury Mallett and asked the sergeant to read him some of the details of the pathologist's report. Hamilton, you bastard, he thought. How much of this do you already know? As he put the phone down, Hamilton rapped on the glass and signalled him to come out.

'What's the matter?' Salter asked.

'They've lost her already,' Hamilton snarled.

'How?'

'They are stuck behind a bloody great lorry in Cranstone, the next village. The lorry couldn't make the turn and *it's* stuck. She didn't even have to try to shake them.

For Christ's sake! Hold on a minute.' He reached into his car and picked up the radio microphone. 'Yes, yes, yes,' he bawled. 'Hamilton here.'

'Suspect disappeared, sir. We have put out a search bulletin.'

'You arseholes,' Hamilton said, and put the microphone back. He turned to Salter. 'She's got a good enough start on them. God Almighty. Now we'll probably have to wait until she comes back and shake it out of her. Oh, those stupid sods. They are supposed to be our best men at this caper.'

Salter was looking through his diary. 'Hold on,' he said. 'While we're waiting, let's take a run into Harcourt Banbury. Not far from here, is it?'

'What for, for Christ's sake? Do some shopping?'

Salter explained. Hamilton listened carefully.

'Give me that diary.'

Salter handed over the racing diary and Hamilton studied it closely for a few moments. 'Right,' he said. 'It's the only steeplechasing meeting she could get to in less than three hours. It's about half an hour away. Worth a try, and a damn sight better than sitting here holding hands with you. We will go and park ourselves by the first fence and see if any plums fall. Hold on.' He spoke into the radio again, giving orders for the men he wanted and what he wanted them to do. 'Well done, Salter,' he said. 'If it works. Got any other bright ideas up your sleeve?'

'Yes,' Salter said. 'But let's do it one step at a time, shall we?'

A good crowd was expected that day, for the card contained a valuable race, the William Hunter Gold Cup Steeplechase, sponsored by the brewery favoured by the Plough. But a good crowd at Harcourt Banbury is no Derby Day and Hamilton's strategy seemed fairly foolproof. Half a dozen men were posted in the area where Salter suggested Rundstedt and Bessell would meet, inside the course by the first fence. At the entrance, two other men were watching the line of cars as they passed on to the course. A green mackintosh was enough identification to spot Rundstedt.

There is only one stand at Harcourt Banbury, but a small building some way past the finishing post, a building which houses a bar and a sandwich counter, has a flat roof where thirty or forty people are allowed to watch the races, and here Hamilton and Salter waited, armed with binoculars that Hamilton had commandeered from the clerk of the course. A dozen other men were posted around the course, all with their glasses trained on Hamilton.

The signal was flashed at fifteen minutes before the first race. Hamilton caught the white glove slowly circling the air. 'She's here,' he said. 'Wait a minute, I'll see if I can spot the car.'

In the distance the line of slowly moving cars broke into two streams; one line peeled off and parked by the turnstiles, the other continued to the gap in the course. 'There she is,' Hamilton said. 'Three cars back from the gate now.'

Salter picked up the car with his glasses as the driver paid the fee for crossing the track, and followed it as it curved out behind the ramshackle refreshment shed in the centre of the field, and reappeared by the first fence. They watched as Rundstedt sat in her car, making no effort to get out and join the crowd. There was no sign of Bessell.

Three races went by, including the big

one. The two men on the roof ate cheese rolls and drank something called coffee out of paper cups, amusing themselves with small bets with each other on the early races.

Then Hamilton asked, 'That our man now?'

Salter trained his glasses on Rundstedt who was standing beside her car, talking to the man Salter knew as Parrott.

'That's him,' Salter said.

'Johnny Bessell, here we come,' Hamilton said, tucking his glasses away in one of his giant pockets.

'Not Bessell,' Salter said, still with his glasses on the couple, feeling like Alec Guinness in Episode Four. 'Cossitt.'

Hamilton fished his glasses out and looked at the pair again. 'Not the laddie you went racing with?' he asked.

'Yes, that's him. But it isn't Johnny Bessell. His name is Cossitt, Michael Cossitt.'

'And who the hell is Michael Cossitt?' Hamilton asked in a friendly tone.

'He is Bessell's former partner in Toronto. He went to jail a couple of years ago. Bessell set him up.'

The loudspeakers announced the runners

for the fourth race and Hamilton waited for the noise to stop, then asked, 'Why did Bessell's former partner kill Bessell's wartime chum? You know, don't you? This is Salter's finest hour.'

'He didn't kill Bessell's wartime chum. He killed Bessell. His partner.'

'Bessell. Not Dillon. Bessell.'

'Yes. Check the morgue. You'll find he has an old burn scar on his upper left arm.'

Hamilton nodded. 'Good, good, good,' he said. 'And what caused that?'

'I don't know. But that's how you can identify him.'

'And where is the mysterious Dillon?'

'I don't know. I haven't got that end figured out yet.'

'Good. I'm glad there's something left for me. Let's go.'

They climbed down from the roof and began to make their way towards the gap where they could cross the track and join Rundstedt and her companion on the inside of the course.

'*Will the riders please mount,*' the loudspeakers said, and a ripple of agitation passed through the crowd which now had only five minutes left to place a bet.

Hamilton and Salter crossed the track in the centre of a small group, and paused inside the rail.

'So what we have here is Mrs Bessell and someone called . . . ?' Hamilton resumed.

'Cossitt.'

'Cossitt it is, then. Getting their own back or blackmailing her husband who was living under the name of Dillon? Right? Bloody impersonator. Right?'

'I think so.'

'Under starter's orders. They're off.'

Salter was struck again with the casualness with which a steeplechase starts, with none of the excitement of a flat race. The first cavalry charge swept down the hill and jumped the fence in front of Rundstedt and her companion. The announcer kept up a steady quiet commentary as the horses disappeared round the bend into the country to begin the first circuit.

'But you don't know where Dillon is?' Hamilton resumed.

'No.'

'I do. He's in a grave up in the Tuscan hills where he died in 1944.'

'Where did you find this out?' Salter asked, after a very long pause. Bas-

261

tard, he thought.

'I haven't confirmed it yet, so you can call it a guess. Ask me another.'

'All right. When did *you* know Dillon was Bessell?'

'Oh, *very* early in the game. We compared the pathologist's report with the army records. And Bessell's brother confirmed that he had been scalded as a child by his mother when she was straining some cabbage.'

'And you've been stringing this out, just to have some fun with me?'

'There is a faller at the ditch.'

'Don't exaggerate your own importance, old chap. I'd have closed this up a long time ago, but I didn't have Cossitt − didn't know who he was until you just told me. My guess was that he was some thug hired by Mrs B. And I didn't know where he was, so I had to wait for her to lead me to him. I filled in the time by watching you. Let's go.'

'The horses are coming into the straight to begin the second and final circuit. Filthy Temper is in the lead, followed by Colonial Boy and Inside Story in that order. These are followed by . . .' and the announcer listed the rest of the horses as they appeared at the

262

head of the stretch.

The ring of plain clothes men had their glasses trained on Hamilton as he waved and moved along the rail. When they were within ten yards of the couple, the leading horses passed them and jumped the fence. Rundstedt looked around at this point and saw Hamilton and Salter bearing down, and shouted out in alarm and began to run away down the rail. Cossitt looked around and saw the ring of police and started to follow her as the police trotted forward. Salter broke into a run but he was too late to prevent Cossitt from ducking under the rail and running across the track in front of the fence. The crowd screamed as a loose, riderless horse, enjoying his freedom, jumped the fence in a graceful arc and smashed into Cossitt with his front feet, then fell across him, pounding his body into the turf.

The rest of the meeting was abandoned, 'owing to the unfortunate accident'. Hamilton had taken charge, sending his men home and helping the first aid attendants to put Cossitt's body into an ambulance. One or two people in the crowd smelled something more unusual than an accident, but the scene quickly dissolved in the English anxiety to beat the crowd home. Mrs Bessell had been caught and taken into custody, and Hamilton and Salter went into the bar, at the superintendent's suggestion, until the rest of the crowd cleared.

'In some ways a bit messy. In other ways, not,' Hamilton said. 'It'll save the Queen a few bob for the trial, anyway.'

'What about *her?*' Salter asked.

'I'm not sure yet. An accessory, of course, but she *might* have been an unwilling one. If she cooperates fully it could go easily with her. Let's go and have a little chat.' He led the way to the office of the clerk of the course, where two uniformed constables were watching Rundstedt in silence.

Hamilton began briskly, explaining to her how much the police knew, and suggesting that providing the remaining information would be helpful to her.

She confirmed that Hamilton and Salter were right in the main, and that the story she had told them in the hotel had been put together by Cossitt.

'He knew we were after him, did he?'

'Sooner or later. It was his big mistake. He knew you would get on to Johnny Bessell, and you would soon have an idea of who to look for. Then he knew that he would stick out like a sore thumb. Especially to him.'

She jerked her head at Salter.

'*What* was his big mistake?'

'Using Johnny's name, in the register and on the postcard. He thought it would be clever to soften Johnny up a bit in advance. Kind of frighten him with his own name.'

'How did he know Bessell was alive, here?'

'We both figured it out. When Michael got out of prison he came back to me and we worked it out. He knew the story of Johnny and his pal, Terry Dillon . . .'

'Dillon died in Tuscany. Right?' Hamilton said, looking at Salter.

'Yeah. Johnny buried him himself. He was his best friend and Johnny decided to keep faith with him. He kept his tags and his paybook in a drawer in his desk at home. He never told the army what had happened because he wanted Terry to stay in the grave he had put him in. When Michael came out of jail we spent a lot of time trying to think where Johnny might have gone. Neither of us believed that stuff about his drowning. Then, when I told Michael that the tags and the paybook had gone — they were the only things that *were* missing— he figured out what Johnny was up to. So he went to Italy and asked around and found out that someone called Dillon had turned up alive, and after that it was easy.'

'You didn't tell the police about the tags and paybook?'

'No, I didn't even realize they were gone until Michael kept questioning me to remember anything that might help us.'

'So you and Cossitt decided to blackmail your husband.'

'Call it what you like, Mister. Johnny screwed me and Michael, didn't he?'

'Why?'

Mrs Bessell blushed. 'Because he caught us. Three years ago.'

'In bed?'

Mrs Bessell shrugged. 'Johnny was the faithful type. He never looked at another woman, he told me, and he couldn't stand people screwing around.'

'So Cossitt sent for you, and you came over and acted as the go-between?'

'Yeah.'

'But Bessell wasn't playing, so Cossitt killed him?'

'I don't know about that. Michael said

they got into an argument. Johnny said we could have a thousand pounds to give Michael a start. But if we tried any more he would go to the police, and take the consequences. Even if he went to jail, his wife would wait for him, he said, and she was more important to him now than anything. He would put everything in her name, he said. He said, too, he could still prove that he hadn't taken a penny of the money Michael went to jail for. I think Michael must have threatened him then and Johnny pulled a knife. But Johnny didn't know anything about fighting and Michael had learned a few tricks in prison. Oh, he killed Johnny all right, but I don't think he meant to.'

Hamilton sat back satisfied and raised his eyebrows at Salter.

Salter accepted the unspoken offer, and asked, 'When your husband caught you and Bessell—three years ago?—did he decide then to do this disappearing act, and leave Cossitt holding the bag?'

'That's right. I didn't know about it then, of course. All I knew was that the bastard wouldn't sleep with me again, but he wouldn't leave me. Till death do us part, he said, whenever I asked him. In the end I just lived with him and did my own thing. He came over here first, right after he caught us. For a holiday, he said. But he pretended to be Dillon seeking an amnesty. Told the authorities he'd been living underground for thirty-five years and now wanted to go straight. He got his amnesty, and all the papers to be Dillon, including a passport.

'He came back to Toronto and spent a year setting Michael up. Then he disappeared, leaving me nearly broke. He'd cancelled all his insurance and took out a big mortgage on the house to put some money into the business, he told them, but it never went into the business. He left just enough in his bank to make his suicide story look good. They took everything to pay the company's creditors.'

'When did he tell you all this?'

'In Boomewood. When he came to my room. He must have already decided he wasn't going to go along with Michael, and I said I'd tell the police. But he told me that if I tried, he had tape-recordings which would prove we'd been trying to blackmail him. Did you find them?'

Hamilton ignored the question. 'Finished,

Salter?' he asked.

The two men stood up. 'Take her into headquarters and tell them to wait for me,' Hamilton said to the two policemen. 'You'll find my sergeant waiting downstairs. He'll go with one of you.'

The two men walked silently out to the parking lot, digesting Rundstedt's story. 'Shall I drop you at the Plough?' Hamilton asked when they reached the car.

Salter came back into the world of two people on holiday. He said, 'What's the time? Stop at the nearest phone-box, will you?'

Hamilton said, 'They'll be having lunch in Toronto now. Better leave it until you get back to the hotel.' He laughed a short bark.

'I want to phone my wife. She's still on holiday somewhere around here.'

When he returned from the phone-box, he said, 'I have to be in Stratford by six. Can I make it?'

Hamilton considered. 'Just,' he said. 'I'll take you. What's the play?'

'Who cares?' Salter said. 'If it's not *Macbeth* it will be new to me.'

During the drive to Stratford, Hamilton

started to snuffle. Salter looked at him in surprise. The superintendent was giggling.

'My game, I think,' Hamilton said.

Salter said, 'Bullshit. You wouldn't have got there today without me.'

'Right,' Hamilton conceded. 'Your point, all right.'

'And I got Rundstedt first, remember.'

'Right again. We'd have got to her soon enough, though. On the evidence of the wanker. It was fairly bloody obvious, except to Churcher, that she was involved somehow. And a short leap from there to wondering about her pal she was shacked up with at the Swan. My only problem was finding him, so I had to put some salt on her tail and wait. You saved us some time on that.'

'And you didn't know that Bessell was Cossitt, did you?'

'I didn't need to, old boy. I knew that Dillon was Bessell. The rest would all have come out in the wash. But I think you did well. Orliff should be proud of you.'

'Considering I was playing with my bare hands against ten guys with over-sized racquets . . .' Salter began.

Hamilton roared with laughter and cut

him off. 'Don't get peevish, old chap. Now, where is this restaurant?'

Salter told him. 'You are not out of the woods, yet,' he added. 'If Rundstedt changes her story back to square one, and gives Cossitt an alibi, just to be awkward – what sort of lawyers do they have in Tokesbury Mallett? – you could spend a lot of time on this yet.' It was a dinky little shot but the best Salter could manage.

'We'll see,' Hamilton said. 'We'll see.'

Over dinner he gave Annie the final chapter of the story.

'Nice timing, Charlie,' she said.

'What?'

'Didn't you notice? The sun has come out.'

It was true. When they left the restaurant they walked out into a superb spring evening. Already the benches along the path by the river looked dry enough to sit on. The world had turned into a travelogue again.

That night, as he sorted out his money, Salter came across the winning betting slip for Montague Road which he would not now be able to cash.

'I have one more call to make on our way

through the village tomorrow,' he said.

'The police station, I suppose. All right. Make it quick.' She stretched herself comfortably under the covers. 'Now come to bed,' she said.

The next morning the sun was still shining and they hurried to be off.

Salter found Sergeant Robey at the desk.

'Why, thank you very much, sir,' he said, when Salter handed over the betting slip. 'I'll put it in the entertainments fund, shall I? By the way, sir, there was a message for you from Superintendent Hamilton if you called.' He took a slip of paper and began reading. 'We found no tapes but we did find a commando knife in the dead man's car,' he read. 'It looks as though he had plans for Rundstedt. She agrees and is very cooperative.'

Salter laughed. 'Give him a message for me, will you, if he calls back? Tell him I've been picking up a little local slang here. Tell him I think he's a jammy bastard, would you?'

'Just in those words, sir?'

'Just like that, Sergeant.'

'Perhaps you'd care to write it yourself,

sir,' Robey said.

Salter wrote the message on a piece of paper and watched the sergeant carefully seal it in an envelope.

'I'll see he gets it, sir. By the way, sir, you do understand? I was only doing my duty. Something the superintendent is very keen on.'

'Oh, I understand, Sergeant. Without you, though, I might have surprised your superintendent. Who knows, I might even have won.'

'Oh, I don't think so, sir. Not against the superintendent. He's very good at this game.'

'That was quick,' Annie said.

'I just wanted to give Churcher my regards. By the way, how was lunch with Mrs Churcher?'

'Fine, Charlie. Just lovely. She's a wonderful cook. Did Churcher tell you he's thinking of calling on you in Toronto?'

For the first time since their arrival, Salter forgot where he was and went round a curve on the right-hand side of the road. He recovered himself and recrossed the line before anything appeared in the opposite direction. 'What do you mean?' he cried. 'Calling on me?'

'He's taking a week's leave, and his wife wants to visit her mother, so he is thinking of taking a charter flight to Toronto. I told her you'd be delighted to show him round and explain your procedures. Hamilton has approved it, apparently. I said he could stay with us.'

'When?' Salter asked. 'When? When?'

Annie giggled. 'Don't panic, Charlie. As Angus used to say in kindergarten, "I'm just joking you." Now listen. I've been looking up some guide-books. There's a little village at the end of the Lake District called Cartmel. Wordsworth mentioned the abbey in *The Prelude.* I'd like to see it.'

'Great. Maybe we'll meet the Ancient Mariner.' One place is as good as another so long as the sun is shining and the pubs are open, he thought.

Annie laughed.

'He's probably running in the fifth race,' she said.

'Huh?'

'They have races next Saturday and Monday. We'll just be in time. We can have a look at the abbey in the morning and go to

274

the races in the afternoon.'

'Jesus,' Salter said. 'It sounds perfect. Now find us a Tweedledum to stay at.'

The publishers hope that this Large Print Book has brought you pleasurable reading. Each title is designed to make the text as easy to see as possible. G. K. Hall Large Print Books are available from your library and your local bookstore. Or you can receive information on upcoming and current Large Print Books by mail and order directly from the publisher. Just send your name and address to:

G. K. Hall & Co.
70 Lincoln Street
Boston, Mass. 02111

or call, toll-free:

1-800-343-2806

A note on the text
Large print edition designed by
Bernadette Montalvo
Composed in 16 pt Plantin
on an EditWriter 7700
by Genevieve Connell of G. K. Hall Corp.